Melodies and Mistletoe

ALSO BY KASEY STOCKTON

Contemporary Romance

Snowflake Wishes

Snowed In on Main Street

Melodies and Mistletoe

Cotswolds Holiday

Regency Romance

All is Mary and Bright

A Forgiving Heart

Sensibly Wed

Pleasantly Pursued

The Jewels of Halstead Manor

The Lady of Larkspur Vale

Love in the Bargain

Scottish Romance

Journey to Bongary Spring

Through the Fairy Tree

Melodies and Mistletoe

KASEY STOCKTON

GOLDEN OWL PRESS

CHAPTER ONE

Hailey Grant scooped up the pile of stuffed animals on the plush living room rug and balanced them close to her chest so she would only have to take one trip upstairs to deliver the things to the toy bin. A dotted ladybug toppled from the pile and rolled across the stark white rug, landing under the fake, snow-tipped branches of the Christmas tree.

Ugh. Gently crouching, Hailey reached for the ladybug and set it on top of the pile in her arms before slowly standing again, her thighs burning. Sheesh. Maybe she needed to add squats to her daily routine. She could slip them in right after her race to get dressed in the morning, shortly before grabbing a granola bar on her way out the door.

Or maybe she could set a new rule for herself: every time she bent to pick up a stuffed animal at work, she would squat. Her butt would look amazing in no time.

Some kids hoarded stuffed animals, collecting them like those spoons people bought in souvenir shops but never intended to use. Those types of kids arranged their stuffed animals pleasantly across their beds without planning to ever play with them. But Kendra was different. Kendra, the six-year-old girl Hailey spent her afternoons chasing around the high-rise New York City loft, played with those little suckers like they were her best friends. And she didn't gravitate toward the type of animals that typically lived on the beds of six-year-olds. No, she loved the *bugs* most.

The fact that they *did* keep her so thoroughly entertained at least made cleaning up what felt like thousands of stuffed bugs every night totally worth it. At least Kendra wasn't into fashion dolls. All those little accessories everywhere would be so much worse.

Hailey paused on the landing at the top of the stairs and peeked through Kendra's open door at the girl's small, sleeping form nestled under the blanket. Oh, please don't ever, *ever* discover fashion dolls.

After the stuffed caterpillars, beetles, and butterflies were all safely stored in the giant bin in the dim room, Hailey took the *Life Cycle of a Butterfly* book perched beside Kendra's pillow and tucked it back onto the bookshelf. She double-checked the latch on the window to make sure it was locked, then let herself quietly out of the room.

Seamless.

It hadn't been this easy in the beginning. Hailey had come to work for the Martinez family when Kendra wasn't even two. It'd been an adjustment, but she'd only meant to nanny for a year or so—however long it took her to get noticed.

But sometimes things didn't work out the way they were so carefully planned. Hailey was *fine* with how her life had turned out so far. She loved Kendra, and the Martinezes paid her insanely well. Of course, her salary was a drop in the barrel that was the immense Martinez fortune. But it was more than enough to keep her stocked in sound equipment and guitar strings. They probably had no idea they were funding such an expensive side hustle.

If moonlighting at bars or producing demos could even be

called a side-hustle. Didn't it have to actually bring in money to earn that title?

The elevator ding rang across the marble floors, and Hailey darted down the stairs, her extra-thick socks padding her silent footsteps. If she hurried, she might make it to Nomad before the band scheduled before her, Midnight Moods, finished their set. And she *had* to be there before they finished, or she was done for. Johnny already told her that if she was late one more time, he'd take her off the docket completely.

But tonight she was prepared. She'd brought her guitar, dressed nice enough for playing in a bar—which, admittedly, wasn't any different from her regular clothes, just a lot more black—and had her Uber app opened and ready to go.

The elevator doors beeped from the Martinezes' foyer before opening, and Amber Martinez stepped into the apartment, her stilettos clicking loudly.

"How was your day?" Hailey asked, sitting on the tufted bench to pull on her boots.

"Fine." Amber waved her hand dismissively. She crossed into the kitchen, visible through the wide, open doorway, and dropped her bag on the center island. "Is Kenny asleep?"

"Yep. She's been out for thirty minutes or so."

Amber nodded. The bags under her eyes and drooping smile highlighted her constant late nights at the office, but she had nothing on her husband. Luis was basically never home.

Hailey leaned down to zip her boots. "Megan had to leave early, so I stacked your laundry in the closet, and she promised to stay late tomorrow."

Amber filled a glass with water from the fridge. "That's fine. I'm sure she'll make up her hours." She glanced over her shoulder, giving Hailey's faded black jeans and boots a once-over. That was all that was visible under the marshmallow-puffy coat Hailey was zipping up. "Where are you heading off to?"

"Just to Nomad." Hailey lifted her guitar case and slung her purse over her shoulder.

Amber's brows lifted. "You've got a gig?"

"I don't know if it qualifies as a gig, but I sing there sometimes."

Amber offered a wan smile. "I want to tell you good luck, but I also never want to lose you."

Hailey used all her self-control to *not* check the time on her phone. She needed to get out of there. And fast. "You know I adore Kendra. It'll take a major recording contract to get me to leave her."

"Good," Amber said. Oddly enough, she sounded super relieved. Thanks for the confidence, boss.

But it was true. Amber had nothing to worry about. The Martinez family wouldn't be losing their nanny anytime soon. Hailey had spent the last four years trying to get her demos into the right hands, and that turned out to be way harder than she'd expected.

"Well, I'll see you tomorrow!" Hailey crossed to the elevator and punched in her key code.

Amber made a farewell-type sound, and Hailey slipped out, hitting the button for the elevator to take her downstairs. Pulse speeding, she wrapped her scarf tighter around her neck and pulled her long, dark curls free. She hitched her bag higher up on her shoulder so she was prepared to run to the corner to meet her Uber driver. This was her last chance to keep the gig and her best shot at being seen. She couldn't lose it.

Declan, the doorman, would give her a scolding tomorrow for running through his lobby, but it'd be worth it. He really was the most crotchety old man sometimes. But hey, he'd been standing sentinel at this building's door for at least a hundred years, so he'd earned himself the right.

A splash of color caught her eye above the doors, and she had to chuckle. Whoever placed mistletoe wrapped in red ribbon up there was clearly a romantic, and it wasn't Amber or Luis. Maybe Declan put it there for a little holiday cheer.

The elevator dinged, and Hailey gripped her guitar tighter, prepared to launch the moment the ancient doors slid open. Light poured through the widening gap as they opened, and Hailey went for it...directly into the man waiting on the other side.

"*Oomph,*" he said, taking the brunt of Hailey's guitar case in the chest.

"I'm so sorry!" Hailey backed up, pulling her case flush against her as she turned to keep walking. She didn't have time to waste. "I didn't see you—"

"No, clearly you didn't," he snapped, checking out his suit and only showing her the top of his head. But guitar cases didn't make messes. It might have bruised his nicely sculpted—nope. Hailey shook her head to stop that line of thinking in its tracks. The guy was still looking down, assessing his designer suit, and didn't appear to notice her walking away.

And the faster she escaped, the better. If this guy planned to claim that she'd snagged his Armani sleeve and required a replacement, he had another thing coming. A perfectly fitted suit like that would probably cost her a month's salary—or more —and Hailey wouldn't put it past anyone wearing something that expensive to pull a jerk move like making her pay for a new one. In her experience, people with money tended to have less kindness or basic courtesy. Or maybe it was an overall igno-rance? Either way, *clearly* the guy was worried about it, or he wouldn't be analyzing his lapel so closely.

Christmas was only ten days away, so she supposed it made sense that she'd run into a grinch at some point.

"Sorry," she called again, slipping outside into the freezing December air. A glance at her phone made her break out in a run toward the waiting car with the Uber sticker on the back window. Twelve minutes. She had twelve minutes to get to

Nomad or she'd be off the docket. With it being her only connection to music at present, it wasn't something she was willing to give up.

She slid into the car and shut the door, settling the guitar case between her knees.

"Hailey?" the Uber driver asked, catching her eye in the rearview mirror. He matched his ultra-hairy picture the app had given her. Someone needed to get the man some beard oil and a trimmer.

She nodded. "Yes, and I'm in a major hurry."

"Who isn't?" He turned his attention to the road and flipped on his blinker.

Well, great. He really didn't sound like he planned to hurry.

She shut her eyes, leaning her head against the back of the seat rest for about a millisecond before sitting up again. It was an Uber, for heaven's sake. There was no trusting the last person who'd sat in her seat, regardless of how clean the driver was. No lice today, please.

The car absolutely crawled down the street, and Hailey forced herself not to beg the driver to go faster. What man in New York City didn't know how to weave in and out of traffic to his advantage? The amount of space the driver left between his car and the one ahead of them had let so many people in, Hailey was positive she could've run across Central Park faster than it was going to take this guy to drive around it.

All the while, the clock ticked closer and closer to the end of Midnight Moods' set.

She leaned forward and rested her forehead on the guitar case nestled between her knees. It would probably be better to prepare herself for losing the gig completely. Johnny wasn't willing to budge, even a little bit, and she should know—she'd already begged her heart out to get another chance, and this was it. He'd been perfectly clear: if she stepped into the bar one second late, she was out.

Her phone glowed in the back of the dim car, the clock changing. Two minutes left.

Was it pathetic of her to hold on to a dream that wasn't gaining any traction? Defeat closed in on her with each passing second as if the world, covered in twinkle lights and draped in red velvet ribbon, was actually dimming outside the car window like a countdown timer.

By the time the car turned onto Columbus Avenue, Hailey was sunk, her vision nearly void of light. Her last connection to the music world was well and truly severed.

Hailey trudged up three flights of stairs in her ancient apartment building and slid her key into the lock, glaring at the broken elevator over her shoulder. By the time maintenance got around to fixing the elevator—if they ever did—her arms were going to be super toned from lugging groceries and guitars up and down the stairs.

She paused. Well, she wouldn't have to worry about that anymore. At least, not the guitar. Johnny, the manager for Nomad, had ended their agreement and hadn't even had the decency to show a little regret. He wiped her from the docket as easily as he'd swiped away drips of alcohol from the bar top; she was sure she'd seen her career flying away as he'd tossed the used rag over his shoulder. Apparently, Johnny was finished with announcing her act then having to apologize for her tardiness.

She didn't blame him entirely, of course. He had a business to run. But would it have hurt to agree to push the gig back a half-hour?

Hailey pushed the door open and dropped her keys in the

bowl on her entry table, then turned and locked the deadbolt. Colored twinkle lights strung down the hallway cast a rainbow-hued glow over her, and she sighed. She put her things down and rounded the corner into the living room. Nikki had *The Hallmark Channel* on the television tuned in to one of the Christmas movies, the only lights in the apartment coming from the movie and the twinkle lights strung on the ceiling and wrapped around the tiny tree sitting against the little window. It was a better view than the brick wall they typically got to see from that window, and Nikki had already threatened to keep the tree up all year just to give their apartment some life.

What did it matter if the tree wasn't actually alive? It was green. But they wouldn't need to keep it up. Little did Nikki know, she had some house plants coming her way for Christmas.

"I thought you were playing at Nomad tonight."

"Nope." Hailey slumped onto the battered sofa and dropped her head back. She closed her eyes, tamping down the defeat clawing at her chest. "Johnny fired me. Or he let me go...whatever they call it when they drop you from a job where you don't actually get paid."

"That punk." Nikki sat bolt upright. "Want me to call his mom? I will."

"No." Hailey chuckled. "Your family connections got me the gig, but it was my job to keep it. And it was my fault I lost it. I was late too many times, and he gave me loads of extra chances. It is what it is, I guess."

"You can't just give up. You told him that your boss gets home late all the time, right? You can't just leave Kendra home alone."

"It's fine, Nik." Hailey gave her a side-eye. "It's not like Nomad was actually going to put me on the map."

"It could have. There's a reason their live music spots are so coveted. Johnny said—"

"Yeah, well, he might brag a lot, but none of the reported music execs that supposedly haunt Nomad approached me, like, ever. So I guess I got my answer."

"*Or* you were just unlucky and never played while any of them were there."

Hailey ignored Miss Positivity and turned her attention to the Christmas movie. A man with a lot of hair gel was on his knees, pleading for a woman's forgiveness. Predictable. He'd messed up. She would forgive him. They'd live happily ever after.

Gag.

"Why do you love these movies so much?"

Nikki blinked. "We've gone over this so many times. Because of all the glorious, beautiful hope that good guys still exist."

Hailey fought the urge to roll her eyes and remind her best friend that these were fake, scripted movies. Instead, she snuggled into the sofa, accepting the bowl of popcorn, and watched the show. When it finally came to a blessed end, a song played over the credits, and she closed her eyes, humming along with the music. She harmonized with the indie-sounding woman singing a redone version of *Silent Night, Holy Night.*

When the credits drew to a close, Hailey continued humming, and Nikki picked up the remote, searching the movies for another one to start. If she was hoping to find one she hadn't seen, she was bound to be disappointed.

Hailey hummed the song she would have finished out the set with that night if she hadn't been late—her big finale. It was slower, softer than her usual beats, but so melancholy and beautiful. If she was allowed to think that about something she wrote. There was something she loved about slow, meaningful music, the kind that gave her chills.

"You know what would be cool?" Hailey sat up, the idea coming to her swiftly. "Taking a fast-tempo holiday song and slowing it down."

"Mmhmm," Nikki said, her gaze riveted by the TV and endless carousel of Christmas movie options.

"No, really." Hailey glanced around the apartment until she caught sight of the Christmas tree and her brain gears spun, working and moving until she lit upon the right idea. "Okay, hear me out." She turned to Nikki and started humming *Rocking Around the Christmas Tree*, getting the tune down before adding the words.

Nikki dropped the remote, closing her eyes and listening to the music while Hailey sang. The beat was slow, drawn-out, and almost harrowing. When she finished, she glanced up and paused.

Nikki's wide-eyed gaze was locked on her. "That was cool."

Hailey swallowed. "Too bad I don't have a producer, or I could pitch them my amazing idea."

"Yet," Nikki said. "You don't have a producer *yet*. Do I have to remind you what's taking over half of your bedroom? I'll give you a hint. It's the reason we can't get another roommate in here and maybe save some rent money."

"Don't diss my sound equipment. It's useful stuff. What we really should discuss is why you can't give up half of *your* room to get another roommate in here." Hailey lifted her eyebrows.

Nikki rose. "Moving on..." She went down the hallway and came back with Hailey's guitar case, dropping it in her lap. "I have an idea."

"What?" Hailey shifted the case and clicked it open, her fingers moving on impulse to pull the guitar from its velvet bed.

"Let's record that song and put it on YouTube."

"Uh, no." Hailey laughed. "I doubt it's in the public domain, and I really don't feel like getting sued."

"Okay, scratch that song. We can find another one." She sat down again and pulled out her phone, the screen glowing over her face.

She was crazy. There was no way Hailey was filming herself

and loading the video to YouTube. Nothing screamed pathetic like wannabes trying to get noticed among millions of other people on the internet.

Nikki's eyes lit up. "Ah! What about *Deck the Halls?*"

That one *would* be kind of cool. Plucking a few strings on the guitar, Hailey picked out a tune and moved it down to a minor key. Adding the words was the easy part, and by the time she finished singing the first verse Nikki was actually bouncing in her seat and clapping, a wide smile spread over her freckled face.

"We're going to be famous!"

"We?" Hailey asked.

But Nikki was already up and going into Hailey's room.

She followed. "Whoa, hey, don't touch anything!"

"I'm just moving the chair," Nikki said. She grabbed a stool from the kitchen and put it in front of Hailey's computer. "This is way more indie. Come on, sit."

Hailey obeyed. "I don't know if this is a good idea."

"Eh," Nikki said, shrugging and powering up Hailey's computer. "What harm can it do?" She got everything in order, then turned on the camera app while Hailey fidgeted with her sound equipment. "Ready?"

Hailey probably looked like a deer caught in headlights, because that was exactly how she felt. But Nikki had a point. No one was ever going to see this video. It would sit on YouTube for a hot minute, get zero traction, and she could delete it in the morning when Nikki was at work. Hailey sat back on the stool, lifting her guitar and strumming a few times. "Ready—"

"Wait!" Nikki ran out of the room and returned with a Santa hat, plopping it on Hailey's head and arranging her dark hair over her shoulders. "I'm glad you curled it today. You've got a perfect wave going."

She'd curled it because she thought she'd be on a stage tonight, but that was beside the point.

Stepping back, Nikki rested against the wall and gave her a thumbs up.

Then she pressed start.

The Santa hat drooped to the side a little, but she focused on the chords and the song, allowing her voice and intuition to lead, shoving away all insecurity and doubt. Music had always had a way of wrapping her in a protective hold, pushing negativity and hardship away and letting her breathe. It was therapy for her. It was life.

When it was over, her body tingled, her fingers itching to begin again. Nikki swirled into action, nudging Hailey out of the way, unhooking her computer from the many cords on the desk and taking it to her bed. Hailey watched with growing dread, knots forming in her churning stomach. She pulled down the Santa hat and flung it at her friend. It was so tacky.

Still. It wasn't a problem. She could take the video down in the morning. It was fine. No one would see it.

Nikki finally glanced up, a broad grin on her mouth. "It's live."

CHAPTER TWO

New York City was way too cold in December. Ryan pulled his coat tighter around his neck, stepping from his sister's apartment building and walking down Fifth Avenue. California had spoiled him with its good weather year-round and chill vibe. He needed to acclimate his habits back to New York—and fast. He'd been a fairly busy guy before moving across the country, but nothing like this. There was no time to sit idle here, not with the company to run and half the employees absent for the next few weeks.

Christmas was really a horrible time at the office. Way too many people with family obligations and extra time off. The office was going to become a dead zone—not a good thing when they had the fiftieth anniversary of *Sound Magazine* and a special New Year's edition coming up that had to be ready to go to press by Christmas Eve.

The whole Christmas Eve deadline was massively unfair when half of *Sound*'s employees were going to be absent for the week leading up to Christmas. But what could he do about it? He hadn't made their schedule for the year. He'd just stepped into it.

Ryan predicted many late nights at the office ahead of him.

By the time he got to the right subway car and found his way to his new building, he was running up the stairs just to warm his body again. Okay, so he could admit it wasn't *exactly* frigid or anything, but compared to SoCal winters, this place was cold.

Sergeant started barking before Ryan had fully gotten his door open. He dropped his messenger bag on the floor, leaning down to rub Sergeant between the ears. "You been bugging the neighbors, boy?"

The mixed-breed mutt tilted his head sideways in feigned innocence. The new apartment was way smaller than they were used to, and it certainly lacked the backyard Sergeant had ruled in SoCal. Ryan chuckled, reaching into the treat jar on the counter, and tossed one to his dog. "Come on, Sarge. Let's have dinner."

Ryan poured dog food into the dish and nudged it over with his foot before pulling out leftover pizza from the fridge to reheat. He turned on his phone. A mass of texts and missed calls littered the screen, and he leaned back against the counter, scanning them for pertinent information. Nearly every notification was from the same person, so he dialed Carter's number and clicked speakerphone. He set the phone on the counter and slid his pizza into the microwave.

"Hello?"

"What's going on?" Ryan asked.

Carter's laugh boomed from the speaker. "You didn't even watch it yet, did you?"

"Watch what?" Ryan lifted a slice of meat lover's pizza and took a gargantuan bite.

"Man, you've gotta watch the video *before* you call me back."

Whoops. Ryan swiped on the screen, finding the message thread with a link to YouTube. He clicked it, and a preview thumbnail showed up of a woman sitting on a stool, acoustic guitar nestled on her lap and a Santa hat over rich, brown waves. She was pretty, he'd give her that. And something about her seemed oddly familiar. Maybe he'd watched a demo of her before? Scanning the screen, he found her name—Hailey Grant. Nope. Didn't ring any bells.

Which meant one thing: he'd given her a pass last time.

Scrubbing a hand over his face, he suppressed an irritated sigh. He didn't have time for this. "Dude, I've been at my sister's house all night, and I'm dead. Can we talk about this tomorrow? You're still coming into the office, right?"

He could almost see Carter shaking his blond head. "This can't wait for tomorrow. Just watch it now. I'll hold."

"Seriously?"

"I'm not kidding, man," Carter said, faintly awed. "You need to see this."

Ryan grabbed his laptop from his messenger bag and set it on the table, shoving another bite of pizza in his mouth while he waited for it to power up.

"Is this girl the next big thing?" Ryan asked, super aware of the skepticism dripping from his voice.

Another garbled laugh sounded through the phone's speaker. "Just watch it."

Ryan found the girl's video, his eyebrows rising as high as the number of views she'd received so far. "When was this posted?"

"Tonight, man. *Tonight.*"

Ryan blew out a low whistle. He checked the time stamp and Carter was right. The video had only been live for three hours and she'd already gotten thousands of views.

"This, my friend," Carter said, smug, "is what we call going viral."

"Okay, I'm watching it now." Ryan hit play and picked up his pizza, folding it to hold in the sausage.

The girl smiled into the camera, and his chest tugged. She seemed different somehow. Self-conscious, maybe? It was refreshing after all the self-absorbed teeny boppers throwing videos up, thinking they were the hottest thing ever. This woman was neither a teenager nor full of herself. He could see that from her smile.

But the *hat*. What kind of woman put up a video in a Santa hat unless she was trying to appear all Christmassy and cutesy? Hard pass.

She looked down as her fingers formed a chord then she began strumming her guitar. It was a slow, simple beat. *Nothing special*, he thought, shoving another bite into his mouth. But when Hailey Grant opened her mouth and began to sing, Ryan leaned in. Was she singing *Deck the Halls?* Yep, she totally was. It was different, though. She'd dropped it to a minor key, and he'd never heard it done that way before. He'd give her solid points for originality, but the choice of song was a bit weird.

Ryan hit the space bar at the end of the song, pausing the video on her smile—now dazzling, like the music had unlocked that extra bit of radiance—before YouTube could begin the next video. He was arrested by the haunting melody still playing in his head. Her voice was so pure, her tone so clean. He was certain he'd never heard her before. Her face rang familiar, but he'd never heard that voice. He would remember it.

He narrowed his eyes, staring at the brunette Santa on the stool. With the video paused, it felt like Hailey Grant could see through the screen, like she was smiling at *him*, and it made him drop his half-eaten slice on the plate.

"Okay, lay it on me," Carter said. "It's great, right?"

"Yeah, actually. It's super original. The stool and the hat had me thinking it was going to be another dumb demo, but she surprised me. Her voice is really something else."

"I knew it. You love her."

Ryan leaned back, startled. Her voice, not her. Carter meant her *voice*. Obviously. Ryan didn't even know this woman. But Carter must have some sort of plan or he wouldn't be bugging

Ryan after midnight. Not when they'd see each other the next morning at the office. "What exactly do you want to do about it?"

"Two words, man: *Ryan Says*."

Ryan scoffed, shaking his head, despite the fact that his friend couldn't actually see him. "No way."

"Come on!" Carter pleaded. "You haven't done one in a while, and the fans will love it. Plus you'll be doing this chick some major favors."

"She's gotten thousands of views in a few short hours. Clearly someone already shared her video on Instagram or something. She doesn't need my help."

"When's the last time you did a video? Before you moved out to California?"

"Yes." Ryan's throat tightened. "At least five years ago. I doubt anyone even follows that lame account anymore."

Carter's voice went higher. "You'd be surprised, actually. I just checked the stats, and it regularly has clicks and views. It could be great for the site. We'll just throw it up, link to it in a newsletter, and boom—you've just made that girl's dreams come true."

He had a point. It wouldn't be hard, and he'd give her a boost. With a voice like that, she deserved a little leg up in the industry. But Ryan was exhausted, and his dry, sandy eyes just wanted sleep.

"Maybe tomorrow—"

"By tomorrow someone else will have found her. These internet sensations rise and fall so fast, if we don't jump on it we might lose our chance. And it could do wonders for the ratings. It'll make Bradshaw happy."

Bradshaw. Ugh. Why did Carter have to go and throw his name out there? But he had a point. Ryan needed to win the man over, and the way to do that was numbers. Cold, hard, excellent numbers.

He looked at the smiling face of Hailey Grant in her corny hat. Her song was so short, Ryan could set up his camera, toss out some opinions, and throw together a video pretty quickly.

He pinched the bridge of his nose. "Fine. I'll do it."

"Yes!" Carter probably fist-pumped the air. "How long do you need?"

"Give me thirty minutes then check your inbox."

"So, since I'm working late, does that mean I can take the morning off, boss?"

"Nope. See you at eight."

Carter laughed. "It was worth a shot. Later, man."

The line went silent, and Ryan clicked his phone off. He carried his laptop into his office, powered on his desktop, and created a split-screen. It took less than ten minutes to set up the recording equipment and his webcam. Drawing in a deep breath, he considered the lovely face of Hailey Grant on his computer.

"You're gonna thank me in the morning," he said, before looking into the camera and clicking *start*.

Hailey woke up with an odd feeling humming in her chest. Something was definitely not right. Sitting up, she glanced around her brightly lit room, gaze dancing across her keyboard in the corner and the wide table full of expensive equipment, searching for something out of place. Her eyes fell on the stool still sitting in the center of the floor. Only now, her laptop rested on it, opened, with a sticky note stuck to the center of the dark screen.

Padding to it in her fuzzy-socked feet, Hailey picked up the sticky note and recognized Nikki's handwriting: *Don't be mad.*

Oh, great. Dread gathered heavy in her stomach. Hailey balled up the note and tossed it on the floor. She made no promises.

Carrying her computer back to her bed, Hailey clicked a button and the screen sprang to life, showing the video she'd made last night and...oh goodness. The sheer amount of views made her heart leap to her throat, her pulse thrumming wildly in her ears. But...the number of likes *did* make up for it a little. She swallowed, scanning the screen until she landed on a suggested video to the side, and her body went cold.

Ryan Says had posted for the first time in years, and Hailey's face was up in the corner of his video. Oh, no. No, no, no. There was no way *Ryan Says* had done a critique of her tiny, thrown-together, podunk video.

Finger hovering over the touchpad on her computer, Hailey stared at the little preview video box, nervous energy shaking her hands. She was not going to like this; she could sense it. So much for assuming no one would ever see this video. Once *Ryan Says* critiqued something, it usually went viral. Except, the guy had been silent on YouTube for the last few years. Why the sudden urge to tear her apart?

To be fair, she didn't actually know if he'd torn her video apart or not. She hadn't watched it yet. And she was clearly stalling now because she was afraid to hear what he had to say.

But putting it off forever wasn't going to make it go away.

Hailey steeled herself and hit play, immediately bringing her hands up to rest on her cheeks. She probably looked like the kid from *Home Alone*, but there was no one here to judge her.

Ryan Says watched his video screen intently as Hailey's voice came through the speakers. She cringed. It sounded fine but knowing a huge music exec was watching her was altogether exposing.

His eyebrows lifted, and Hailey dropped her hands, gripping the blanket haphazardly strewn beside her. He was clearly surprised by something, but was it good surprised, or bad surprised?

"This is interesting," *Ryan Says* said. "You take the set-up of the girl with the guitar, the Santa hat, and the Christmas song, and you immediately assume she's going to bust out a whiny, metallic song. But her voice is rich. It's got depth. There's an element here that makes it unique, but I need to listen more to put my finger on exactly what that is."

"Okay," Hailey said to her computer screen, her heart pounding. "Then close your mouth and listen."

He seemed to hear her. His gaze flicked to the camera then back down before he paused Hailey's video. "Now, if you'll notice here we have a bit of raw emotion showing through. If she was properly trained, this would be much more controlled."

Hailey's blood heated. What right did *Ryan Says* have to criticize her at all? She hadn't asked him to do this. For all he knew, she was being intentionally raw. Whatever that meant.

"But once again, let's revisit that rich depth I referred to earlier. There is something about her tone that is"—he circled his hands as though fanning the air would find the words he was missing—"well, it's unique. Different from anything I've ever heard before. If she had a unique song, too, then maybe this video would be worth watching—"

Hailey slammed her computer closed. No washed-out music theory major (or at least she *hoped* he had some sort of music degree) had a right to tell her how intentional her rawness was.

Nikki was going to pay for this.

CHAPTER THREE

Hailey walked down the sidewalk, cinching her scarf tighter as the phone rang in her ear.

Nikki answered the call almost right away. "How much do you hate me right now?"

"I could never hate you—"

"Oh good." Nikki sounded relieved.

"Just don't blame me if you get home later to find your tiny tree bare and your twinkle lights missing."

Nikki gasped. "You *wouldn't*. What did Christmas ever do to you?"

Hailey ducked underneath the scaffolding over the sidewalk. "It's not Christmas I'm trying to get revenge on."

"Yes! I'm getting the extra ramekins, Chef." Nikki's voice dropped. "I've got to get back to work. Just tell me you're planning to call the guy."

"Call who?"

"Hailey! You watched to the end of the *Ryan Says* video, right?"

"Of course not. The guy was a jerk. I don't need that negativity in my life." She reached the Martinezes' building and lifted her hand in a wave at Declan, before moving to the elevator at the far end of the lobby.

"Just watch it to the end," Nikki said. "And then call the guy! Gotta go."

The phone beeped in her ear, indicating the call had ended, and Hailey stood before the elevator, staring at the keypad that would give her access to get up to the Martinezes' loft.

She should just let it go. It would be healthier if she let it go, right?

Oh, who was she kidding? Curiosity nipped at her, and she opened her browser, locating the video.

Her voice came through the phone, soft and low. Then Ryan's voice reached her ears. *"This is interesting. You take the set-up of the girl with the guitar, the Santa hat…"*

Scrunching her nose, Hailey scrubbed forward, skipping the rest of the video until she reached the end. Her song had ended and Ryan, with his dark eyes and chiseled jawline, was speaking into the camera. He probably thought he was so hot. He wouldn't be wrong, of course, but that was beside the point.

"So all that aside, I've got a proposition for you, Hailey Grant."

She froze, lifting the phone closer to her face. Ryan directed a lopsided grin at the camera. His voice was husky, and his eyes lazy, slightly tired, which, she supposed, could be owed to the super late time stamp on the video. Annoyingly, it only made him more attractive.

"I know this is a long shot. But Hailey, I've got a gig that needs a performer. If you're interested, get yourself to the *Sound Magazine* offices in New York City by the end of the week. If not" —he shrugged—"well, a guy can take a hint." He winked at the camera, and the video ended.

Hailey scoffed. *Ryan Says* actually had the gumption to wink at her after critiquing her singing voice and lack of professional training?

"Miss Grant," a wary voice called from behind her, and she jumped.

The ancient doorman—complete in his crisp uniform and old-fashioned bellhop hat—approached her slowly, concern creasing his face. "Is the elevator giving you trouble, dear?"

Her cheeks warmed. How long had she been standing there, watching her phone? She reached forward and punched her code into the command box, and the arrow lit up, which meant the car was traveling her way. She lifted her phone. "I was distracted."

"Ah." Declan nodded in understanding. "Of course. I don't know how you young people get anything done these days with those devices always in your hands."

The elevator beeped, the doors sliding open, and Hailey stepped inside. "Have a good day, Declan."

He dipped his head in the old-fashioned respect that fit his uniform well. "The same to you, Miss Grant."

It was too bad chivalry was a thing of the past. If more guys would act like that, maybe Hailey would have more interest in dating. Not that she had the time for it. Well, maybe now that her career had screeched to a complete halt at Nomad last night, she *would* have more time for dating.

Unless…unless her career *hadn't* ended, and she took *Ryan Says* up on his offer. What kind of gig did he have for her? That was the real question. Hailey tapped her short nails against her phone screen as the elevator dinged, and the doors opened. She tossed her coat, shoes, and purse into the closet that practically disappeared back into the wall then went in search of Kendra.

She didn't know what she was going to do about the proposition. But she had ten hours ahead of her with Kendra, and she couldn't do anything about it during that time anyway.

"I have to run." Amber whirled into the kitchen, her heels clicking across the marble floor. "I told you my brother just moved back to New York, right? Well now we've got a huge ad meeting for the company tomorrow and he's stressed, so we have to go over numbers today." She rolled her eyes. "It's not like I don't have my own magazine to run or anything. And it's almost Christmas. Why now?"

"So you think it might be a late night?"

Amber groaned, wrapping her scarf around her neck. "It better not be. No, it won't be. I haven't tucked Kenny in all week. Tell her to count on seeing me tonight."

Hailey nodded, and she hoped she wasn't going to be lying to the poor girl.

"Kenny's in her room, and there's a list of things she needs to get for a school project in her backpack. It's due tomorrow." Amber roughly pulled on her coat and buttoned it over her scarf. "I would've ordered them already, but I just learned about it this morning."

"Don't worry. We'll get it taken care of."

Sweeping her purse off the counter, Amber shot Hailey a grateful smile and her footsteps clicked away from the kitchen and into the entryway. "Thanks, Hailey. You're a peach."

A peach? Was that a good thing?

Hailey turned to ask Amber if she'd already fed Kendra breakfast, but the elevator doors closed, leaving a still, empty silence behind. It wasn't a problem though. If she could get Kendra ready for school in the next ten minutes, they could stop by that delicious bakery they both loved and have cronuts for breakfast. Flaky, buttery, fried dough drenched in icing was exactly what Hailey needed right now to get the YouTube critique and the stupid-handsome guy who did it off her mind.

Ryan pulled his computer from his messenger bag and set it on the cafe table, powering it on. The little bakery was just around the corner from his sister's apartment, and totally out of his way, but he'd stopped here after dropping some files at her place a few days before and had eaten the best breakfast sandwich he'd ever tasted.

He'd returned two more times since. If he wasn't careful, he was bound to become a regular. Not that he minded, but his waistline might. At least in New York he walked pretty much everywhere while his poor car sat unused. Hopefully, health-wise it would all even out.

The dark-haired waitress brought over his plate with a side of orange juice, and he smiled his thanks while she adjusted her elf hat. Now, to get to business. He opened the reports Bradshaw would want to see tomorrow and scanned the numbers for the thirtieth time. Nope; they still hadn't magically improved overnight.

Sighing, he scrubbed a hand over his face. Carter was right. They needed to do something to become more relevant in this ever-advancing tech world, and they needed Bradshaw's advertising account to do it.

Ryan's phone rang loudly in the little shop, and he pulled it out, answering it right away. He slipped his AirPods into his ears and waited for them to connect.

"What's up, Carter?"

Carter's voice was high, a mocking falsetto. "I've got a gig for you. Come to my place of business if you want a leg up in the music industry."

"What are you talking about?"

His voice returned to normal. "Did you ask a YouTuber out on a date over YouTube? Be honest."

Yes, he had. But he wasn't about to admit it now. "You saw the memos Sarah sent around for the anniversary party yesterday. We don't have a band yet...to celebrate a *music* magazine. I may have just filled the spot."

"Or maybe that girl lives in Montana and wants to spend Christmas with her family and not travel across the country for a stab in the dark chance to perform for a stranger who asked her out online."

"When you say it like that you make me sound like a creep."

Ryan could perfectly imagine Carter's brows raising.

"Well, I don't know if you meant to do this or not," Carter said, "but you've *flooded* the lobby with music hopefuls. Security formed them into a line, and it goes out the door. We're gonna have Manhattan cops shutting it down soon and citing us for lack of crowd control."

"Are you kidding?" Ryan's mouth hung open. He thought telling her to come to the office was smart—he hadn't posted his phone number or anything, and his secretary would be able to tell by her face if she was Hailey Grant because she'd been on video.

"Do they all look like the girl in the video?" he asked.

"Not even close. I don't know how they think they're gonna fool you. But it's getting bad. You better get down here."

"Hang on just a second." Ryan stood up, downing his orange juice in two gulps. He closed his computer and shoved it back in the bag before taking out his wallet and dropping a bill on the table. Swinging his bag over his shoulder, he took the sandwich from the plate and spun toward the door. What had he been thinking?

Okay, so he knew what he'd been thinking, but he could also admit to himself that it wasn't reasonable. He'd been attracted to Hailey Grant. But not in a creepy way. She was beautiful, obviously, but her *voice* had drawn him in. He'd felt suspended listening to her. Yeah, she could use a few lessons on control, but she had a gift.

You could teach music theory and development. You couldn't teach God-given talent.

And Ryan wanted to meet her. Maybe he'd made his proposition sound more like he was asking her out, but…well, okay. So he might have been asking her out. But he'd tried to save it by turning it into a joke at the end. Hailey Grant probably had a boyfriend anyway, and they probably watched the critique together, laughing at the pathetic attempt Ryan had made to meet her.

At least the gig he'd offered was real.

"You there, man?" Carter asked, his voice loud in Ryan's ear.

"Yeah, just gathering up my things. I'm heading your way."

CHAPTER FOUR

The cutest part about Kindergarteners was how large their backpacks were in comparison to their small bodies. Hailey reached forward and tugged Kendra's ponytail out of her coat, and her charge glanced over her shoulder, taking another bite of her banana as they walked down the sidewalk.

Hailey wasn't the *worst* nanny in the world. Life was all about balance, and this banana would balance out the fried, sugary cronut they were about to have.

"Can we get hot choc—"

"Chew," Hailey gently reprimanded, and Kendra snapped her mouth closed, chewing her bite quickly.

Kendra swallowed. "Can we get hot chocolate?"

If the banana was meant to balance the cronut, what was going to balance hot chocolate?

A man walking toward them on the sidewalk was focused on his phone and veering their direction. Hailey slipped a hand over Kendra's shoulder and guided her out of harm's way. Maybe he shouldn't be texting and walking at the same time.

That was it! Walking. Walking would balance the hot chocolate. They had to travel two blocks past the school to get to the bakery anyway.

"Sure, Ken."

Kendra beamed, shoving the last of her banana in her mouth and handing Hailey the peel. Of course there were no garbage cans around when she needed one.

"I'm heading to Target after I drop you off to get the supplies for your project. What kind of ornaments did you have in mind for your All About Me Tree?"

"Insects."

"Ah, I should have known! Who wouldn't want spiders crawling all over their Christmas tree?" She reached forward and crawled her fingers over Kendra's head like a spider.

Kendra giggled, cringing. "Spiders aren't bugs. They're arachnids."

Hailey threw her arm over Kendra's shoulder and pulled her in tight. "What's the difference?"

"Insects have three body parts. Spiders only have two."

"They still have eight legs."

Kendra looked up, her tiny, dark eyebrows pulling together. "What does that have to do with anything?"

"It makes them gross," Hailey explained, tossing the banana peel in the garbage can on the corner. She opened the bakery door, the heat from inside the building clouding over Hailey on the sidewalk. Kendra rolled her eyes and moved to step inside, but a man barreled out of the bakery and slammed into her. He did a quick step to the side, but a croissant flew out of his hand, plopping on Hailey's chest before it slid to the ground, leaving behind a greasy, white sauce. Gross. She pulled Kendra close to her side before turning her attention to the man, and—*Ryan Says*. Her entire body stilled.

What were the chances she'd run into *Ryan Says* in a tiny bakery in Manhattan?

"Send them home, Carter," he said, staring at her with intense, hazel eyes, his dark hair swept to the side.

Huh? How did that make any sense?

"Just tell them I've found her," he said. "Because it's the truth."

Okay, was he crazy? Hailey tightened her hold on Kendra, pulling her closer to her side.

Ryan Says stuck his hand out as if Hailey would actually shake it. "Hi. Ryan Bierman. Nice to meet you in person."

"Uncle Ryan!"

Uncle *what*?

His face dropped to Kendra, confusion on his brow until his eyes lit up. "Kenny?"

She pulled free from Hailey's protective arms and leaped toward the YouTube critic, throwing her arms around his waist. He returned her hug, then pulled AirPods out of his ears. "What are you doing here?"

Shouldn't Hailey be the one asking questions? At least she knew he'd been talking to someone on the phone…probably.

Kendra didn't have the same reservations. "We're getting cronuts and hot chocolate before school."

"Yeah?" Ryan asked. "That sounds like a healthy way to start your day."

Wow. So he was judging her caretaker skills now, too?

"Have you tried a cronut, Uncle Ryan? They are donuts and croissants mixed together and they're amazing."

"I haven't, but maybe I need to."

"I don't know if it's a good idea," Hailey said, unable to help herself. "It's not a healthy way to start your day."

He glanced up sharply, his hazel eyes widening. "Oh, I didn't mean—I wasn't saying…" He cleared his throat. "Are you two together?"

"Of course we are, silly." Kendra beamed.

"Do you want to introduce me to your friend?" His voice softened, his attention on his niece.

She turned. "This is Hailey, my nanny."

He straightened.

"You must be Amber's brother." The pieces clicked together so suddenly, Hailey felt like an idiot for not having figured it out sooner. Amber had mentioned her brother moved back to New York—the brother who co-owned Bierman Media, one of the biggest media companies in New York City. Was *Ryan Says* a YouTube name for Ryan Bierman, the media mogul? He'd kind of been absent from the internet for years.

And never once had Amber talked about him in any specific sense. In Hailey's defense, she spent all her time with Kendra, not her parents.

"Yeah, I'm Amber's brother. How long have you been working for her?"

"Four years."

"Whoa." Ryan ran a hand through his hair, stepping back. "It's weird that we haven't met before now."

"Not really. They only see you when they fly to California, right? I've never traveled with them." Amber's mom came up from Florida more often than not and visited them here, so they didn't have a lot of reasons to leave.

"I can't believe..." He shook his head. "How long have you been singing?"

Any chance that maybe he hadn't recognized her went out the door. Except, they were still standing in the doorway. "I don't really have time to chat. I need to fill Kendra with sugar and grease before I send her to school."

"Okay, listen, I didn't mean—"

"Uncle Ryan, we can't be late. Then I won't earn any stars today."

"We don't want to get in the way of your stars, do we?" He looked at Hailey. "Can I walk with you?"

Kendra glanced between her uncle and her nanny. It was unfair of him to ask this around the kid. It wasn't like Hailey could say no, could she? The guy was Amber's *brother*. Kendra had confirmed it.

"Sure." She gestured inside, and Kendra skipped into the building.

"I'll meet you out here. I need to call the office. Oh, and Hailey?"

"Yeah?"

"Sorry about the..." He pointed to her chest, swirling his hand around the air like he was at a loss for words. "I didn't mean to throw my sandwich at you."

"It was an accident." Hailey hurried after Kendra, letting the door close behind her. She placed their order with a barista dressed as an elf, adding an extra-large hot chocolate for herself just to show Ryan how little his health comment meant to her. The elf handed over their cronuts, and they moved to wait for their drinks. Taking a stack of napkins, she tried to wipe most of the gunk from her coat, but the giant grease stain from his sandwich was only spreading. Oh, come on. This could not get worse.

"Uncle Ryan just moved back to New York, and it made Mommy really happy," Kendra said, taking a bite of her cronut.

Hailey paused, turning toward her young charge. "Yeah, I bet. It's always nice when family can be nearby." Would it be considered inappropriate to pump Kendra for information about her uncle? Hailey could probably Google him, but this source was much better and way more reliable. Probably.

She glanced at the long, glass windows at the front of the shop and watched Ryan pace, his expression animated like he was talking to himself. Well, he probably *was* talking to someone in those tiny buds in his ears, but they weren't immediately noticeable, so he just looked funny. Like one of the men who paced in the subway at night, shaking his hands at invisible enemies.

"Daddy said that Uncle Ryan just needed to get some directions, and Mommy told him to be nice." Kendra took another bite of her cronut. "But I don't know why that's mean. I ask for directions at school, and Miss Holmes is always happy to help me."

"It's not mean. Asking for directions is a perfectly acceptable thing to do, Ken." Which is probably not what Luis meant when he said that about Ryan. He probably meant that the man needed some direction in his life—or that would be Hailey's guess, at least. It made her curious to find out why.

"Two hot chocolates!" The barista in the elf hat put their to-go cups on the counter.

Hailey checked the time then reached for the cups, handing the small one to Kendra. "Okay, we have eight minutes. We've got to hustle. Can you eat and walk fast?"

"I'll try," she said valiantly.

They went outside, and Ryan fell into step alongside them as they turned up the street.

"How far is the school?"

"Two blocks," Hailey said.

Kendra ate her last bite of cronut and licked her fingers before tentatively taking a sip of hot chocolate. She stopped on the sidewalk, turning her stricken face on her uncle. "Oh no! I ate the whole thing! I was going to let you try a bite."

"That's okay, Ken. I can get one next time I go."

Her face brightened. "Or you could try Hailey's if she says it's okay."

Gee thanks, kid. Hailey smiled at Kendra's hopeful, shiny eyes and lifted her pastry bag to Ryan. "You can have it."

He laughed. "I'm not taking your cronut."

"Have you really never had one?"

His face creased into an apology. "I'm afraid I haven't. I have heard of them before though."

"Well, think a croissant, like the one you threw at my coat—"

"Okay, okay…" He threw up his hands, chuckling.

"—but deep-fried and covered in icing."

"It sounds delicious."

Hailey reached into her pastry bag and ripped the cronut in half, offering a piece to him. "Try it."

"Thanks." Ryan accepted the pastry, winked at his niece, and took a bite. "Mmm. This really is good." He shoved the rest in his mouth, and Hailey made herself look away. Even the way he ate was attractive, highlighting his strong jaw.

This was not good. She could not find Amber's brother attractive. The guy was wearing a designer suit and…wait. She sized him up, trying to imagine how he'd appear if all she could see was the top of his head as he analyzed his chest.

It added up. Same suit, same build, same bulky biceps straining against the coat sleeves. The guy had been heading right for the Martinezes' private elevator. This *had* to be the rude man she'd run into last night.

Kendra chatted in between sips of her child-sized hot chocolate as they traveled the last block to the school then handed Hailey her empty cup. She hugged Ryan, and he kissed the top of her head. "Have a good day, Kenny. I'll see you later."

"Today?" she asked, her bright eyes betraying her hope.

"Probably not today, but soon."

"Okay. Bye, Hailey!" she called, turning to run into the school's small, gated yard.

The teacher latched the gate behind Kendra, and Hailey passed Ryan, searching the street to find a trash can. She hadn't even had a sip of her own drink yet, but her stomach would probably resent it now anyway. She needed to get a good distance from Ryan so she could breathe again.

"So, what are you doing now?" he asked, his hands resting casually in his coat pockets.

"I have some errands to run for Amber."

"Oh, you're an assistant, too?"

"No." She spotted a trash can down the way and started toward it. Maybe if she was lucky, he wouldn't follow her.

Darn. She wasn't lucky.

"Then what are you to Amber?"

Slipping the remaining half of the cronut into her purse for later, she tossed Kendra's cup in the trash and took a sip from her own. Mmm. Okay, so hot chocolate *was* nice in the morning. It slowly warmed her core from the inside. Facing Ryan, it was hard not to notice his sculpted cheekbones and direct gaze in the crisp morning light.

"I'm her daughter's nanny. Everything I do is for Kendra."

Ryan narrowed his hazel eyes. "Why do I have the impression you don't like me very much?"

Uh oh. Had she been super obvious? Time to backtrack. "I don't know you well enough to like you or not."

"That really didn't answer my question."

She raised her eyebrows, taking another sip of her drink. A woman walked by, pushing a wide jogging stroller, and Hailey moved closer to the street to give her room to pass.

"New question," he said, stepping to the side with her. He ended up uncomfortably close. "Why do I have the impression you really don't want to be my friend?"

"Maybe you should look internally for an answer to that question." There. That would confuse the heck out of him, and it wouldn't get her in trouble with her boss. But seriously? What was this guy thinking? She turned around and started walking, sipping more of her drink. It was settling nicely in her stomach, despite her earlier worry, and warming her frozen fingers.

"Hey, wait." He jogged to catch up. "Seriously, I don't get it. I help you out, and this is how you treat me?"

She halted, causing Ryan to bump her with his shoulder; her drink sloshed at the impact, spilling hot chocolate on her hand. She sucked air through her teeth, immediately wiping her hand on her pants to remove the sticky liquid.

"Sorry."

"Forgiven."

"So easily?" he asked. "You're hard to figure out."

"Tell me something. Did you go see your sister last night? Like around ten?"

"Yes."

She stared at him, blinking slowly. "Did you run into anyone in the lobby?"

"No. Wait…" Recognition lit his eyes. "Was that you? The woman that bolted out of the elevator?" He put a hand out. "Okay, I know I was being rude then, and I don't have an excuse. I was frustrated, it was the end of a really long day, and I had just come from an important client dinner…"

"You always decide how you choose to treat people, and it shouldn't be something that varies depending on circumstance."

"Oh, come on, Hailey."

"Listen, these"—she pointed to the mess on her coat and the hot chocolate stain on her hand—"were clearly both accidents. Calling me out on the internet and pointing out my flaws was intentional. So no, *Ryan Says*, we are not, and never will be, friends."

CHAPTER FIVE

Ryan could not have been friend-zoned harder—and by a woman who didn't even want to be his friend. He rounded up all the attraction he felt and did his best to throw it into a bucket of ice water because this woman clearly did not like him. Though, how she could possibly have taken *anything* negative away from his YouTube critique flummoxed him. He'd been blown away by her voice. Had she not watched it? She really hadn't seen his admiration?

Her green eyes were blazing, her lips flat. The December cold was pinking her cheeks in an attractive way. Or, maybe that was her anger.

Well, Ryan had said in the video that he could take a hint, and she had just delivered one on a semi-truck. Except, she hadn't said anything about his offer. "What about business colleagues?"

She tucked her chin, lines forming on her brow. "What?"

He'd surprised her. Maybe that was a good sign. "The gig I offered you. It's still yours if you want it. I'm not asking to be your friend or anything. We can have a strictly professional relationship."

Hailey's calculating eyes roamed over his face. "You're serious."

"Of course I'm serious. We need someone to play for the fiftieth anniversary party of *Sound Magazine* on New Year's Eve. The song you performed is perfect for the event. How many similar songs do you have prepared?"

"None."

Now it was his turn to be surprised.

"I threw that together in half an hour and my friend posted it online. We weren't expecting to get any kind of reaction."

He was satisfied to learn that he'd pegged her correctly after hearing her sing. Of course his initial thoughts when he saw the hat and the stool weren't kind, but he'd keep those to himself. "So could you come up with more music that's similar? Christmas songs redone, I mean."

"I could, but…I don't know." She lifted her cup and sipped from it. She'd sipped the giant cup of hot chocolate no more than three or four times, and he wondered if she'd ordered such a big one just to spite him. Given her current reaction, he wouldn't put it past her.

"What if I give you the day to think about it and you can let me know?"

"Yeah, I guess that would work."

She seriously wasn't jumping at this chance of a lifetime? Ryan tried to understand her hesitation, but he couldn't. "Okay. I'll expect to receive your answer by the end of the day."

She nodded, appearing unsure. He pulled his card from his wallet and flipped it over. Then, taking a pen from his bag, he wrote his cell number in black ballpoint. "I look forward to hearing from you."

She quirked an eyebrow at him, and he chuckled. "Think what you want, but I really am a nice guy."

"I'll believe it when I see it."

"Then give me a chance to let you see it."

Hailey didn't respond to his blatant flirt, and he didn't blame her. She'd told him she wasn't interested, and it was immensely disappointing. Instead, she tucked the card into her purse and turned to walk down the sidewalk. He stood there and watched her go, refusing to check the time. Carter had probably called him forty times if the incessant buzzing on his watch meant anything; he could only hope they had managed to clear the Hailey Grant wannabes out of his office.

Halfway down the block Hailey dropped her cup in the garbage can and kept going until she disappeared around the corner. Yep. She'd totally bought that drink just to spite him. And despite himself, he couldn't help but grin.

The sky was dimming beyond the windows and Ryan was tired of being in the office. He'd arrived at *Sound*'s building in time to watch security escorting a few stragglers from the lobby, and he'd been grateful he hadn't had to deal with that.

Note to self: don't put an offer like that on YouTube—or any internet site, for that matter—ever again.

Carter had been a champ though. If he'd really been worried about it, he could have edited that last ten seconds out of the video.

A beep preceded his secretary's voice on his phone's inter-com. "Your sister is on line two."

"Thanks, Karen." He pressed the button, then clicked the speaker option. "Hey, Amber."

She sighed, blowing static into the speaker. "Can we resched-ule? I promised Kenny I would tuck her in tonight, and I haven't done it once this week. I really need to be home."

He pinched the bridge of his nose, leaning his elbow on the glass top desk. "The meeting with Bradshaw is tomorrow."

"Yes, and I feel fully prepared. Everything for *my* magazine is in order."

"But I don't."

"Ryan, this is why we have a board. So that you don't have to do this sort of thing alone."

"But it hasn't been doing great, which is why I moved home. I'm not going to move across the country and then give a half-effort to reviving the magazine. I want to be prepared for everything Bradshaw throws at us. We *need* this ad account."

"Then meet me at my place. We can hold the meeting after I kiss Kendra goodnight."

He dropped his hand, staring at the phone. That could work, and he might have a chance to see Hailey again. She hadn't called him yet...not that he'd been checking his phone every five minutes or anything.

He cleared his throat. "Sure. What time?"

"Eight-thirty? Nine?"

"Deal. I'll see you then."

Ryan hung up the phone when a knock came on his office door.

"I'm just heading out," Carter said, slipping inside the room. "I've got Janica Harper lined up for a photoshoot Tuesday, and Sarah's team will handle the interview. It's the perfect cover for the New Year's edition."

"That's fantastic, but won't it be cutting things a little close? Everything has to be finalized by next Friday. That only leaves us three days."

"My team is on top of things. I think if everything else is ready by then it should be fine. Did you read Sarah's email yet? She outlined her ideas for the interview."

"No, but I trust her. I'm sure it'll be great."

Carter stepped further into the room, dropping into one of

the chairs on the other side of Ryan's desk. "She thinks the feature should wait to go live on the website until a week after the magazine is released."

"But we always release it the same day."

"Which gives readers no motivation to buy the hard copy. I see what she's getting at here. You *did* send out that email asking for revival ideas."

"True. I'll read it and think it over." He leaned back in his chair. "I don't know if I'll have the brain capacity for it until the meeting with Bradshaw is over."

"Have you checked the numbers for your *Ryan Says* video? That should help."

He nodded. "Let's hope so. If we don't get this ad funding we can't expand the digital platform." He rubbed his temples. "I don't really want to be the Bierman who lets the magazine fail right after its fiftieth anniversary. My grandpa and my dad will be shaking their heads at me from heaven."

"If they're really watching you, man, then they know you've been in California the last five years."

"Exactly. I ran away, and the magazine fell apart."

"Listen, no one expected you to stick around after your old man passed. Running this place wasn't your dream. I saw that; your dad saw that. When you got the offer to work for Remmy Records, everyone understood why you accepted it. Your dad would say the same thing if he was still around."

"You can't actually know that, but I appreciate you trying."

"This isn't the only thing in Bierman Media he ran, Ryan. Your dad cared about this place, yeah, but he diversified for a reason."

"Ding dong!" Sarah said, simultaneously knocking and letting herself into his office.

Ryan saw his secretary standing behind her, giving him a helpless gesture. He may have only been back for a few weeks, but even he knew there was no stopping Sarah from getting where she wanted to be.

Her blonde ponytail swished behind her, and she paused behind the second chair facing his desk. "Oh, hi Carter. I didn't know you'd be here too. Good thing I have two left." She grinned at him, her eyes lingering a moment too long before dragging them over to Ryan. "Just wanted to bring you a little peppermint bark to start your weekend off right."

She held two white-and-red-striped boxes out, one toward each man, flashing her bright smile at them.

"It's Thursday," Carter said, taking the box.

That didn't dim her smile. "Yes, it is. But I'm working from home tomorrow, so I won't see you before the weekend. I have a meeting with Janica Harper's publicist working out the details for the interview. I wanted to catch you before you left, and I'm *so* glad you're both here because I have a great idea for the shoot."

Ryan set the box of peppermint bark on his desk and motioned for Sarah to be seated.

"Vivi Meier shared a photo last night of the view from her terrace, and it was clearly the New York skyline." She looked between the men like this should mean something to them. When neither reacted, she continued. "If she's staying in Brooklyn and she'll be around Tuesday, it would be incredible to invite her to the shoot. Janica can still have the cover and the feature, but we could throw some shots in of the duo together. Ten years ago they were a major hit, and the people who followed them then are reading our magazine now."

Ryan leaned his elbow on his desk, running a hand over his mouth. It wasn't a bad idea. The tricky thing would be convincing Vivi Meier to participate without giving her a major spotlight.

Carter looked less convinced. "Last I heard they still weren't speaking."

"They don't have to speak to take some photos. They're performers. This is what they do, and they haven't been seen together in the last ten years, so this will be huge for their fan base. It helps everyone. It'll bring eyes to us, which will make Janica's spread more of a success and get her higher recognition, and it could revive interest in Vivi, which has lagged the last few years."

"It will be making a huge statement," Ryan said. "You have my permission to broach it with the publicist, but if it raises any red flags, abandon the thought immediately. We can't afford to lose Janica Harper right now."

"Deal," Sarah said. "People are going to freak seeing Cali Girls reunited." She turned to Carter. "Do you want to meet in the morning? We can go over the artistic points for the shoot before I propose them to Janica's pub."

Carter fixed a smile on his face. "I thought you were working from home tomorrow."

"I am. I have a guy coming to begin my bathroom remodel so I need to be there, but you could meet me at my apartment. It shouldn't take too long."

Ryan leaned back in his seat and enjoyed the indecision crossing over his friend's face. Yeah, Carter was the Art Director, and his input could probably build a case for bringing Vivi Meier. But the guy clearly didn't want to go to Sarah's house.

Was there something going on here that Ryan didn't know about? He'd gotten to know Carter well when they both started at *Sound* ten years before, and they'd stayed friends after Ryan left for California. He was absolutely going to drill Carter the moment Sarah let them be.

"How early?"

Sarah glanced up, thinking. "Nine? I just need my notes ready by the meeting, which should start at eleven."

"Okay, I'll be there." Carter's mouth was set in a firm line, but that didn't seem to dampen Sarah's enthusiasm. She stood, grinning, her heels clicking over the wooden floors as she left.

Sarah had left the door open, but Karen, Ryan's secretary, got up and shut the door, her round face creased in an apologetic smile. Karen had been at *Sound* almost as long as Ryan's father had worked there. She was likely thinking of retiring in the next few years, but Ryan hoped she'd be around for a while. He remembered when her face was less lined with age and she would slip him a wrapped peppermint candy, the soft, round kind that melted on his tongue.

"She's determined to get back together, man, and I just can't let myself go there again."

Ryan sat up. "*Back* together? When did you guys date? This is the first I've heard of it."

Carter leaned back, stretching his legs out under Ryan's desk and rubbing his forehead. "It was like two years ago. And it just didn't work out. I don't like dating women I work with. Then they're everywhere."

"Yeah, that's terrible," Ryan agreed, his tone dripping with sarcasm. "Who wants to be able to see their girlfriend all the time?"

Carter looked up, his fair eyebrows lifting. "The fact that I didn't want to see her all the time was a good indicator that it wasn't meant to be. I don't regret the relationship...okay, well, yeah. I regret it. I feel like we just got into a groove being friends again, and now she turns around and pulls something like this. I feel horrible. I know I'm going to have to disappoint her tomorrow."

"Just don't screw up the deal with Janica Harper."

"Sarah's too professional to let anything get in the way of her job." Carter stood, stretching. "Well, I'm off the clock now. You still meeting with your sister?"

"Yeah, later tonight. I'll probably go grab some dinner and head over there after."

"Good luck with that. You want my opinion?"

"You'll probably give it to me either way."

Carter grinned, showcasing a row of straight, white teeth. "Bradshaw is going to give us the ad account. He has a long-standing relationship with Bierman Media, and his relationship with your Mom goes back longer than you've been alive. Our numbers have already gone up since you did your *Ryan Says* video last night, so I really don't think you have much to worry about."

"You're probably right." Ryan checked his phone. Nope; still nothing from Hailey Grant.

"I usually am," Carter called, stepping out of the office. He swiveled at the door, leaning against the frame. "Hey, did that YouTube girl ever call you back about the gig?"

"No. I'm starting to think she's not interested."

Carter chuckled. "She didn't jump at the chance when you found her at that cafe, so I'd say that's a safe assumption."

"Go home," Ryan said, laughing. His friend threw up a salute and left. Karen gathered her things and waved goodbye before leaving, too, the office growing quieter as the employees drifted out. Pulling open a new tab on his computer he found Hailey's video and pressed play.

Goosebumps spread down his arms at the sound of her voice, and he closed his eyes, letting the music drift around him, spreading comfort over his body. As the final strains of her song came to a close, he checked his phone. Disappointment slid over him.

Still nothing.

CHAPTER SIX

"Time to brush your teeth," Hailey said, taking the little plastic praying mantis from Kendra's small hand and setting it on the kitchen table.

"No, not yet! Just two more bugs?"

"How about you go get fully ready for bed, and then you can glue two more bugs before I tuck you in."

Kendra paused, tilting her head to the side. "I thought my mom was going to tuck me in tonight."

Hailey pasted on a smile. "She might. Let me call her while you brush your teeth."

"Okay!" Kendra hopped up, skipping from the dining room. She jumped up the stairs one step at a time. Amber hadn't texted yet to say she would be late, so Hailey was hoping she would arrive soon.

The elevator dinged, indicating that someone was coming, and Hailey closed her eyes in relief. Amber was a good mom, but she was a busy one. These moments she spent with Kendra were so important for both of them.

"Hello," Hailey called after the second ding came. "How was work?"

Ryan stepped into the dining room, his hand casually holding the strap of his messenger bag, his shoulders glistening from rain. "It was fine, thanks."

Surprise clenched her stomach. "Oh, sorry. I thought you were Amber."

His mouth tipped in a half-smile. "No worries. You know what would have made my day better?"

"If you hadn't lost your sandwich on my coat this morning?"

His smile widened. "Yeah, actually. Or if this girl I asked to play for my company party would have just called me and accepted the gig."

She dropped her gaze to the plastic bugs piled on the table. She should take the gig. A chance like this would never come again. But her pride was ugly and huge and getting in the way of making the wise choice. The guy had been mean—his words had hurt. Making him suffer and *not* giving him what he wanted was not her best move, but it felt so pleasing.

And if she was being completely honest, the idea of singing for a room of people who worked in the music business when one of them had just called her out for being untrained gave her anxiety.

She looked up and caught his gaze. "I figured you would take my silence as an answer."

Pulling his bag over his shoulder, he hung it on the back of a chair and started unbuttoning his coat. "Can I at least ask why?"

"Scheduling conflict." She wasn't about to tell him that the grandiosity of the event frightened her. She was used to playing in bars, not filled event centers celebrating the fiftieth anniversary of an old family business.

As much as she hated to admit it, Ryan had been right in his critique. She had never been formally trained beyond classes in high school in her small Connecticut town. She was underqualified.

"You can't change it?" he asked.

"I don't see how. I've already been scheduled to work that evening so Amber and Luis can go to the party."

"Darn." He sat on the chair opposite her at the table. "I hadn't thought of Kendra. Do they not have another babysitter?"

"They've never needed one. Not since I started working here, at least."

Small lines formed between his eyebrows. "Do you never have time off?"

"I don't really need it, but I usually take a few days off when your mom comes to visit."

"Well, I'll talk to my sister—"

"Please don't." Hailey's heart lifted, filling her throat. She never would've balked at playing a large event before—this ridiculous self-consciousness was not typical for her—but she couldn't help it. She had Ryan's voice in her head on repeat saying how much better she could be with proper training. There was no way she was going to agree to sing for a party of professionals who worked in the music industry.

Her old self—as in, the literal Hailey of yesterday—would've jumped at this chance. It was too bad he hadn't offered her the gig *before* he'd saddled her with this crippling self-doubt.

"I know we can find someone—"

Kendra started down the stairs. She saw her uncle and moved into a run. "Uncle Ryan! Why are you here? Are you tucking me in tonight?"

He swept his niece into a hug, turning her on her side and tickling her tummy. Between bouts of glorious children's laughter, he explained. "Your mom told me it was really important for her to be here tonight to tuck you in, so we decided to have our meeting here. Is that okay with you, Kenny?"

"Yes!" She crawled out of his arms, her cheeks flushed and eyes glowing. "Want to see my About Me Christmas Tree?"

"Of course I do."

She pulled the half-decorated tree over toward her uncle and spun it slowly.

"Wow," Ryan said, drawing the word out. "That is...something else. I love all the different bugs you used. It's very original."

"I was supposed to decorate it with something I love."

"It looks great."

She beamed under the praise. The elevator beeped, and Kendra jumped, running from the room.

"Why the bugs?" Ryan asked the moment Kendra left the room. "I thought she'd outgrow that by now."

"I think her insect infatuation has only grown over the last few years."

"Thanks for the info. I'll store that away for Christmas."

"Her favorites right now are blue morpho butterflies and praying mantises. Get her a gift based on either of those, and she'll love you for life."

"And you?" he asked.

"I'm not telling you what I got her for Christmas. You'll steal my idea."

He held her gaze. "I meant, what gift would make *you* love me for life?"

She crossed her arms over her chest, leaning back in her chair. Did he really just say that? How many ways did she have to reject the guy? Maybe if she cataloged the ways he had broken her spirit and her confidence he would get the hint.

"Oh, I know." Ryan mocked deep thought, tapping his finger against his chin. "I could set you up with the chance to sing in front of an enormous room of people who work in the music industry. Oh, wait..."

He could not be serious. Amber's and Kendra's voices trailed into the dining room; the Martinez women would shortly be in the room. Hailey swallowed the bitterness on her tongue. "Yeah, maybe I would be able to take you up on that incredibly gracious gift if *someone* hadn't recently told me that I needed proper training."

"Wait, I didn't say—"

"Can we finish the tree tomorrow?" Kendra asked, bounding into the room before her mother.

"I'm sorry, sweetie, but we have to take the tree to school in the morning. Maybe I can glue the last few bugs on it for you. Then they will be totally dry by tomorrow."

She shrugged. "Okay. My mom is going to read me a story now. Goodnight, Uncle Ryan." She rounded the table to give him a hug, then did the same for Hailey.

Amber slipped off her coat. "Thanks, Hailey. Ryan, I'll be down in twenty."

"No worries. I've got all night."

Amber looked relieved and followed her daughter up the stairs. At least Kendra had forgotten about her deal to glue two more bugs on the tree before bed. Hailey took out the glue and globbed it on the body of a black beetle before securing it to the branch and holding it.

"I think we need to talk about this video." Ryan sat up in his seat, and Hailey could feel the weight of his gaze on her, but she kept her focus on the bug. Fifteen more seconds and she could release the gross little plastic thing.

"There's nothing to talk about."

"You are clearly upset about it." He scoffed. "But I don't get why. I was doing you a massive favor."

She glanced up sharply. "I didn't realize I should appreciate being put down."

"Being put down? I did nothing but praise you. And my account has a major following, even after being dormant the last few years, so you can thank me for a few thousand views."

Hailey released the beetle and chose a ladybug next, spinning the tree to find a good, empty spot. Globbing glue on its belly, she stuck it on a branch. "*Nothing* but praise me?"

"Yeah."

She had to work hard to refrain from rolling her eyes.

"You seriously don't think I was praising you? Hailey, your voice blew me away."

She let go of the ladybug, picked up a centipede, and pointed it at him. "Pull up the video."

"What?" He sounded incredulous.

"You want me to prove it? Pull up the video."

Singing floated their direction from upstairs, Amber singing to her daughter, and Hailey directed her attention back to the bug. She only had three left before the tree would look filled in and she could leave.

Hailey's song sounded through the speaker of Ryan's phone, followed shortly by his commentary. The air in the room was stiff, fraught with strained energy, and Hailey kept her attention on the bugs.

"This is interesting. You take the set-up of the girl with the guitar, the Santa hat, and the Christmas song, and you immediately assume she is going to bust out a whiny, metallic song. But her voice is rich. It's got depth. There's an element here that makes it unique, but I need to listen more to put my finger on exactly what that is."

"See?" Ryan said. "Compliments."

"Now, if you'll notice here we have a bit of raw emotion showing through. If she was properly trained, this would be more controlled. It wouldn't jump all over the place."

"More controlled? Jump all over the place? Ryan, you told me I needed training before I could be taken seriously. If you were comfortable saying that in a video on the internet with massive reach, how do you expect a room of trained musicians to feel about my voice? No." She stood, leaving the last few bugs off the tree. Kendra could keep those to play with. "Thanks for your magnanimous offer, but I won't be playing your event."

He shut his phone off and stood, following her into the foyer as she opened the closet and pulled out her coat. "You are holding on to one minor critique? You didn't even hear the praise, did you?"

The praise? No, she hadn't really heard the praise. She'd been too busy smarting from the criticism. Gripping her coat, she turned, locking onto his gaze. "How am I supposed to hear anything positive when you pinpointed my greatest fear about myself, calling me out for the untrained fake that I am?"

"Okay, slow down. You can sing and play, so you aren't a fake, and there is nothing wrong with being untrained. You have a gift, Hailey."

She closed her eyes, her mom's words pressing on her mind. *You've got a gift, Hailey. God doesn't hand out talent like yours every day.* It was impossible to grow up hearing that all the time and not begin to believe it. So she'd skipped applying for a musical school, thinking she could work hard and make her big break in New York. After years of trying—and failing—to make any headway, she'd begun to doubt her choice. She had a gift, right? But if she had a gift, why was no one interested in her demo?

Because she had never been properly trained. Why would a producer pick her up when there were fifty other girls who sounded just like her, but had been coached into perfection?

"I don't have more songs prepared, and I don't think I have enough time to come up with any."

"You told me you threw that song together. I think you can do it. And besides, the party is on New Year's Eve so it shouldn't be all Christmassy anyway."

"Why do you care so much? Why are you pushing this?"

He took a step closer, his eyes slightly narrowing. Dropping his voice, he held her gaze, his breath caressing her cheek. "Because I think you deserve a chance to make something of yourself, and I can give you that chance."

A shiver ran down her spine. "What about the negative voices in my head? What should I do about those?"

His breath seemed too shallow, his eyes darting between

hers. "Focus on the praise, Hailey. Listen to my video again. Listen for every good thing I said, and *then* give me your answer."

Hailey swallowed. He smelled heavenly. Whatever expensive cologne he wore was worth every penny.

"Will you do it?" he asked. "Will you listen again before you make your mind up?"

She nodded, not trusting her voice.

Ryan stepped back, and Hailey reached for her shoes, slipping them on before swiftly pulling on her coat. She drew in a deep breath, catching a hint of his scent as he gave her more space.

"Good luck with your meeting," she said, nodding toward the dining room.

"Yeah, thanks."

Hailey punched her code into the elevator keypad and the door immediately opened. She wasn't sure she could get out of there fast enough. The room had grown thick with tension, her attraction to the critic only developing the longer she spent time with him.

She turned around, leaning against the back wall as he stood in the foyer, his hands in his pockets and his face void of emotion, watching her. The doors closed on him and her eyes drifted shut, ignoring the mistletoe hanging in the elevator and what it made her want to do.

She was in trouble. She had a strong feeling her attraction to Ryan wasn't going away anytime soon. If she listened for the praise in his video like she promised, it was bound to increase. And that was no good.

CHAPTER SEVEN

Nikki sat on the couch with a bowl of popcorn and a Hallmark movie on the television, a peppermint-scented candle burning on the kitchen counter. This scene was such a regular occurrence during December that Hailey thought nothing of it. She liked Christmas, and she loved that her roommate made their home feel so festive.

Hailey dropped her purse on the counter and went to sit next to Nikki in the dim living room. "What a long day."

Nikki paused the movie, shifting on the couch to face her. "What happened? Did you contact *Ryan Says*?"

"No. He found me."

"*What?*"

"I know. I ran into him outside of the Corner Bakery. You're never going to believe this."

"Ugh tell me! I hate it when people say that. It just postpones knowing even longer."

Hailey grinned, tempted to drag it out. But she didn't. "*Ryan Says* is Ryan Bierman, brother to Amber Bierman Martinez, and uncle to Kendra."

Nikki's mouth made a perfect circle. "No."

"Yep."

"What the actual heck?"

"I know. I got into it with him about how rude his critique was—"

"Rude? He loved your voice."

Even Nikki thought that? Maybe Hailey should really give him another chance. "I just heard him point out how untrained and flawed I was."

"Yeah, I think it's human to fixate on flaws. But I wouldn't hold that against him. He's been downright blunt in some of his old videos."

"Most of them."

"Precisely, and he was nothing but uplifting in yours."

Hailey wouldn't say those words exactly. "He made me promise to listen to his critique again, to look for the praise and then make my decision. But it's hard. I mean, I don't know if I have the guts to sing for such a large event. The gig he offered me was for *Sound Magazine*'s fiftieth-anniversary party."

"Shut up. Are you kidding me?" Nikki bounced on her seat, her gaze flicking to the stack of *Sound Magazines* sitting on their coffee table surrounded by Nikki's editions of *Food Weekly*. "That's like if Gordon Ramsay asked me to cook for a dinner party of his favorite restaurateurs. You *can't* turn this down, Hailey. It's a once in a lifetime chance. Think of all the doors it could open for you."

"Or think about how Ryan could be right, and I'm *not* trained, and it'll be obvious to all those well-trained ears."

"You can't let yourself think about that. It's dangerous. You can either give it a shot or give up."

But giving up didn't really feel like an option, either. Hailey opened her phone to the video and hit play, leaning her head against the back of the sofa and closing her eyes. She was a woman of her word, and she'd told Ryan she would listen again for the positives. So, she did. And the longer the video went on, the more she realized that both Ryan and Nikki made good points.

She would be an idiot to turn this down. Even if most of the room could detect her untrained voice, if there was a chance that one person would like her enough to overlook it, she should try.

Sitting up, Hailey closed out of YouTube before the video ended and opened a new message box. She typed in the number Ryan had written on the back of his card then sent him a message.

Hailey: *Okay, I will graciously accept your offer on the condition that Amber can find someone else to watch Kendra that night.*

The three little dots showed up right away to indicate that he was typing, and her hands shook, her heart pounding. What *would* Amber think of this? She'd only said a few days ago that she didn't want to lose Hailey to a music career.

But Hailey's answer held true. It would take a major offer from a label to get her to leave Kendra.

Her phone buzzed.

Ryan: *Deal.*

Ryan: *Amber can figure something out.*

Hailey: *You should let me work that out with my boss myself.*

Ryan: *Cut a guy some slack here. I'm just trying to help.*

She felt duly chastised. He wasn't wrong. He'd done a lot for her.

Hailey: *Sorry. Thank you.*

Ryan: *You're so unbelievably welcome.*

Hailey: *A little humility wouldn't hurt, you know.*

Ryan: *I have to go. The woman I'm meeting with is giving me nasty looks.*

Hailey chuckled. She could picture Amber's irritation perfectly.

She turned to Nikki. "Hey, you got any plans on New Year's Eve?"

"Just catering some swanky uptown party. Why?"

"Want to take the night off and babysit Kendra? You'll make like three times as much as you do catering."

"You only make twice as much as me."

"Yeah, I was thinking *I* could pay you extra to make it worth it."

Nikki rolled her eyes. "You don't have to. I'd love to babysit. I've always wanted free rein in the Martinezes' loft. Wait!" She gasped, scooting closer on the couch. "Did you take the gig?"

Hailey couldn't temper her smile. "Yeah."

Nikki squealed, throwing her arms around her friend. "You're going to be famous!"

Ryan set the phone on the table, unable to curb his smile.

"Why do you look so happy?" Amber asked, her eyebrows drawn in confusion. Her eyes brightened. "Is it a girl?"

"No. Well, yeah, but not the way you think. Hailey just agreed to play *Sound*'s anniversary party."

"Hailey? You mean *my* Hailey?"

"Have you heard her sing?" Ryan asked, leaning back in his seat. "She's good, Amber. Like really good."

Amber didn't look pleased. Her eyebrows pulled together, her mouth pinching into a line. "Why would you do this to me? Do you realize how much we rely on her?"

Ryan paused, leaning away from the table. Of course they relied on their nanny, but they must care about her and her success more than that. His sister wasn't a monster.

"You know she's been with Kendra since she was a baby, right?" Amber's voice grew more serious. "Kenny doesn't even know what life is like without Hailey in it."

"She'll probably never have to know life without Hailey in it. I can't really see that woman walking away and never looking back. But you know Hailey won't be your nanny forever, right?"

Amber narrowed her eyes. "Why? Maybe she will. You don't know how well we pay that girl. She will never leave us for another job."

"But she might for a career." Ryan *knew* Hailey was going places. He'd sensed it in his bones the moment he'd heard her sing. He had a gift for sniffing out talent. It's what had gotten him a job with Remmy Records to begin with.

Luis stepped into the room, his dark hair disheveled and his suit coat unbuttoned. He set a brown leather briefcase on the table and scrubbed a hand over his eyes. "Why is December the busiest time of the year?" He glanced up and seemed to notice Ryan for the first time. "Oh, hey man."

"In *your* line of work?" Ryan asked. "Probably because people need support in order to face their family."

"You have no idea," Luis said, shooting them a brief smile. "But I don't discuss my patients."

Which had always been a disappointment to Ryan, since his brother-in-law was the psychiatrist for some pretty high-powered people, evidently.

"How about your daughter?" Bitterness dripped from Amber's tone. "Will you discuss that? Because Ryan is trying to steal her nanny."

Luis's eyebrows shot up. "You have a kid we don't know about, Ryan?"

"All I did was offer her a chance to play for *Sound*'s anniversary party and now Amber's freaking out." His eye caught on the small fake Christmas tree at the end of the table covered in plastic bugs, and he itched to pull out his phone and text her again. But he had nothing important to say. He just had a strong desire to speak to her. "You can find someone else to watch Kendra that night though, right?"

Luis shrugged. "Maybe my sister can take her."

"Your sister?" Amber shook her head. "I'd prefer someone sober, but thanks for the idea. Hailey can figure it out. She's already agreed to work, so if she wants the time off then she'll have to get a replacement."

"Someone we trust," Luis said.

Amber looked more and more annoyed. "If we're finished going over numbers then I'm calling it a night." Her chair legs scraped against the marble floor. She closed her laptop and carried it from the room.

"Don't mind her. She just doesn't like change." Luis didn't bother following his wife. "It's not like you'll actually take the nanny from us. It's just one night."

Ryan knew this about his sister, but he disagreed with Luis. There was a chance this *would* take their nanny, and Amber knew it as well if her reaction was any indication. "Have you heard her sing before?"

"No, but I don't see her much." Luis seemed untroubled by this fact. "Kendra adores her though, so I think she's doing her job well enough."

Oh, he had no idea. Ryan stood. "I better get going."

Luis rose and reached to shake his hand. "It's good to see you, man. How's the adjustment back to New York going?"

"I miss the warmer winter in LA, but it's good to be home."

"If you ever want to chat about the change, just let me know. I can put you in direct touch with my secretary."

Ryan nodded, holding back his amusement until he reached the elevator. Luis wasn't one to hand out free advice. He was a professional, and a go-getter. There was a reason he could afford an apartment overlooking Central Park.

His old family money was one of those reasons, of course, but his success had something to do with it, too.

Ryan's apartment didn't look over the park, but he had a pretty decent view of New York at night, and he wasn't complaining about the location. Then again, his ambitions had never been as high as his sister's or her husband's. Ryan just wanted to do something that made him happy, that filled in the space in his chest that loomed empty and hollow.

He'd followed his father's footsteps in business working for *Sound* until the opportunity to work for Remmy Records had taken him out to LA, but as much as he enjoyed the production side of music and rubbing shoulders with artists and producers he'd long admired, it never quite filled his missing pieces. He hadn't yet reached satisfaction.

And the trouble was, he still didn't know what he was missing.

CHAPTER EIGHT

Ryan wanted to throw something. All that stress, effort, and worrying about being prepared in time for the meeting, and Bradshaw had to go and push the meeting back. By *two weeks*. Ryan read the email again, sipping at his glass of water before setting it back on his kitchen table.

I'm heading out of town for the holidays, so we need to reschedule. If January 2nd works for you then send a message to my secretary, and she'll get it on my calendar. Merry Christmas Biermans.

The little note at the end was an annoying touch. If Bradshaw knew he had holiday plans, why had they scheduled the meeting for the week before Christmas? Ryan closed out the screen and shut his computer. He sent a text to Amber to make sure she'd seen the email and picked up Sergeant's leash.

"If we don't have to be at the office for a meeting, we're going for a run."

Sergeant barked back like he was in full support of this plan.

Running was a good idea. It would vent all of Ryan's extra irritation. And maybe they could run past the Corner Bakery in time to see his favorite niece and her nanny grabbing breakfast.

He had been such an idiot to comment on the health factor of the cronuts before. Kendra was a kid, and Ryan highly doubted that Hailey filled her with sugar every single morning before sending her to school.

This belief was confirmed when he hung around the bakery, ordering his sandwich and eating it outside with Sergeant, with no sign of Hailey or Kendra.

He was tempted to run past the school but pulled his phone out instead. He wasn't planning on stalking Hailey and Kendra. He just wished he could see them.

But how did he ask if they were out walking around without sounding like a stalker? He changed his tactic.

Ryan: *Do you have a demo tape?*

Hailey: *No, but I have a demo CD and a digital copy. I live in the twenty-first century.*

He chuckled. Okay, so clearly he hadn't meant a legitimate cassette tape. He started back toward his apartment, typing as he kept Sergeant on a short leash.

Ryan: *Will you send it to me?*

Hailey: *That depends on what you're planning to do with it.*

He just wanted to hear her voice again...but that explanation would make him sound like a creep. He could be a professional.

Ryan: *I want to get an idea of your range and abilities. No pressure. I promise not to distribute it.*

Hailey: *You're welcome to distribute it if it lands me a record deal.*

Ryan: *Noted.*

Hailey: *I have to run home and start some wassail after I drop Kendra off. I'll send it over then.*

Ryan stopped on the sidewalk and glanced behind him. But, no, he was too far away now for an *accidental* bump into her. He should have just walked by the school.

Ryan: *Any cronuts today?*

Hailey: *No, actually. We were going to go on the way to school, but then this tiny voice in my head reminded me that it was too much sugar in the morning. So I got her an ice cream instead.*

Ryan laughed. She was joking. Right? Of course she was. She had to be.

Ryan: *Very funny.*

Hailey: *In all seriousness, thank you for offering this gig to me. You didn't have to do that, and I really do appreciate it. Even if I'm terrified.*

Ryan reached his building and started up the stairs, letting Sergeant climb ahead of him. His pulse thrummed, pounding in his ears, and he ran the last set of stairs, eager to sit down and give his phone proper attention. He wanted to reply with nonchalance but not flippancy. Punching in the key code on his front door, he let himself inside and unclipped Sergeant's leash.

The last time he'd put this much thought into texting a woman was over two years ago. And *that* inter-office romance had only lasted eight months. It would've been much shorter, too, if he'd just had the gumption to end things. But when dating within the workplace, it was important not to ruffle too many feathers. Speaking of, he really should text Carter to make sure the guy was going to survive the meeting with Sarah. But first, he needed to respond to Hailey.

Ryan: *You're welcome. And I get why you're stressed, but you don't have to worry. You're going to do great.*

The three little dots never showed up, so he sent another text.

Ryan: *Also, what on earth is wassail?*

Hailey: *You're joking, right?*

Ryan sent a GIF of a man looking awkward and stepping back, disappearing behind a tree.

Hailey: *It's Christmas in a cup. Like hot apple cider but with a citrus tang. You boil it on your stove or in a crockpot, and it makes your entire home smell like the holidays.*

Ryan: *It sounds like I've been missing out.*

Hailey: *You have. I'll send you my grandma's recipe.*

Ryan imagined himself stewing apple cider over the stove and laughed. The idea of *Hailey* doing it, however, was charming.

Tossing Sergeant a treat from the countertop jar, Ryan went to shower. He needed a long, hot steam and a reminder that Hailey wasn't into him like that. She couldn't have been clearer, and he would do good to remember it.

Hailey dropped the cinnamon sticks into her crockpot and stirred the mixture, leaning down to sniff it. She didn't know why she did that. It wouldn't smell great until it had had time to simmer. Which was fine, since she'd be out of the apartment until later that night. She only wanted a little something to make her apartment feel like home during the holidays, since she wouldn't be going home to her parent's house in Connecticut until Christmas Eve, and that was still a week away. She checked the time on the stove. Shoot; she needed to hurry. She had to get back to the Martinezes' house to do Kendra's laundry. At least when she got home from work her apartment would smell absolutely divine.

Nikki tore into the kitchen, grabbing her water bottle from the counter and filling it up with the fridge's water dispenser.

"What are you working today?" Hailey asked, gathering the orange peels and empty apple juice containers to throw away.

"We've got a company lunch at the Marriott and an employee holiday party in Chelsea."

"Isn't that a lot for one day?"

"Yeah, but it's the holidays." Nikki shrugged, tightening the cap on her water bottle. "All this extra work will pay for that course I wanted to take on macarons."

"Oh yes, please take that course. And then practice a lot."

Nikki put on her coat. "Maybe you can bring Kendra by next week and we can make those Santa graham cracker things we used to make with your mom when we were kids."

"The ones with the coconut beards? That's not a bad idea. I'll run it by her."

Nikki smirked. "You think a six-year-old is going to refuse frosting and M&Ms?"

Hailey bumped Nikki with her shoulder. "No. And I think it'll help Amber and Luis feel more comfortable if we get you two together before you babysit."

Nikki looked stung. "I've been around Kendra before."

"I know this, and Kendra knows this, but her parents probably don't remember."

Nikki grabbed her small backpack purse and strung it over her shoulder. "Keep me posted on *Ryan Says*. I want to hear any developments."

Like how he had been texting her that morning for a demo? Oops. She'd almost forgotten to send it. She waved goodbye to Nikki, wiped down the sticky counter, then went to email her demo to Ryan.

His sudden interest was almost alarming. Good thing she'd shut him down already. It was already hard enough to be around the guy without letting any feelings get in the way. He was on a whole different level than she was. Lowering herself onto the chair at her desk, she considered her green sweater and jeans, her plain brown waves, and nondescript green eyes.

Ryan was designer suits and a razor-sharp jawline. Hailey was oversized sweaters and a round little nose. Whatever fantasies skated through her mind when she thought of the man were inappropriate and unsafe for her mental state.

She found the file, attached it to an email, and sent it off to the address she'd gotten from Ryan's business card.

Three songs. She'd sent him two covers and an original to

show her range and style. Hopefully, it was enough to make him feel like he had made the right choice in asking her to sing for his company party.

CHAPTER NINE

The only thing in the Martinezes' living room that spoke of Christmas was the enormous fake, snow-tipped Christmas tree and the pre-lit garland over the hearth strewn with silver ribbon. Their home was the epitome of simple and tasteful, but it lacked the magic of handprint ornaments and the smell of home-baked gingerbread men and a crockpot of wassail on the counter.

Hailey pulled her knees up on the couch, balancing the notepad on her legs. She tapped the pen against her lips, reviewing the song list she'd already practiced. It had been three days since she sent Ryan her demo, and he'd had nothing but good feedback for her. Such strong approval, in fact, that she'd started to wonder if she was being pranked. Could anyone like her voice *that* much?

Either way, everything was falling into place except the song list. Her column of practiced, comfortable, appropriate songs was short. Like, four songs short. And the column headed with *Ideas* was ridiculously empty. But nothing was coming to her.

"Hey, Kendra," she said, gathering the girl's attention from the rug where she sat surrounded by her fuzzy little stuffed bugs and butterflies. Remnants of the peanut butter and jelly sandwiches they'd eaten for lunch stained her cheeks. "What's your favorite Christmas song?"

"*I Want a Hippopotamus for Christmas.* Or maybe *Jingle Bells.*"

Well, *Jingle Bells* was too Christmassy for a New Year's Eve party, and Hailey didn't know if she could sing about hippos at such a swanky event. Maybe if she mellowed it out enough. "Do you think your mom and dad will like hearing that song at their fancy party?"

Kendra nodded seriously. "Of course. Who doesn't love that song?"

Right. Who? Maybe if she mellowed it out, dropped it to a minor key... She cleared her throat, hummed an intro, and tried it out. Kendra watched, her hands clutching a praying mantis and a large stuffed spider.

It actually didn't sound terrible. It was an old, classic song. She finished up then tipped her head to the side. "What do you think, Ken?"

A deep voice answered behind her. "I love it."

Hailey startled, but she didn't need to look over her shoulder to know it was Ryan behind her. Why hadn't she heard the elevator beep? She really got lost in her own little world when she sang, and not always in a good way.

Kendra squealed and jumped up, running around the couch. "Uncle Ryan! Did you come to see me?"

"Of course I did. Whoa, did you know you have a spider on your hand?"

Kendra giggled. "It's not *real.*"

He flashed a handsome smile. "Oh, right. How silly of me. So, was your nanny just singing a song about a hippo?"

Kendra took him by the hand and led him toward the couch. He slipped off his coat, revealing a light blue button-down shirt tucked into navy slacks, and Hailey had to avert her eyes from the way his arms strained against his sleeves. He wasn't super built or anything, but he clearly worked out. And his clothes fit him really, really well. Like well enough to outline his toned muscles.

"Can I get another song preview?" he asked when Kendra made her way back to her mountain of plush bugs on the rug and began lining them up.

Hailey pulled out her peppermint Chapstick and applied a layer. "I don't have my guitar."

His gaze dropped to her lips, then lifted to her eyes. "That didn't stop you a second ago."

Hailey's heart thudded against her chest. She swallowed, hoping she sounded casual. "Were you aware that both Amber and Luis are at work right now?"

There was a glint of a challenge in his narrowed eyes. "Yeah."

"Great. So what can Kendra and I do for you on this fine Monday afternoon?"

The house was quiet but for Kendra's soft humming of *I Want a Hippopotamus for Christmas* while she lined up her toys.

Ryan cleared his throat. "I needed to invite you to a sound-check next Thursday night at the Granger Studio. It's in the West Village and should only take about twenty minutes or so."

"You couldn't text me that information?"

"I was heading home anyway, so I figured I'd stop by and deliver the invite in person." He leaned in, quieting his voice. "And this way I get to see my favorite girl."

Her heart fluttered, breath catching in her throat. Ryan's gaze tripped over to Kendra. *Chill out, Hailey. This guy is not into you.*

"What time next Thursday?" she asked, her voice sounding higher than normal.

"Nine. It's kind of late so I'd be happy to give you a ride."

"You don't have to do that. It's not that late." Had he chosen the time so she'd be able to make it after work? He knew how late his sister stayed at the office most days.

"I don't mind."

"Really, it's fine," she said. "What's the point of getting the monthly subway pass if I don't use it?"

He gave her a funny look, then nodded. Clearing his throat, he leaned back on the sofa, stretching his arm out over the back. "I also wanted to say that you could bring your boyfriend to the soundcheck if you want."

Hailey glanced up, catching his eye. He was watching her so intently, she had a moment's temptation to take him up on his offer. But since she hadn't had a boyfriend since high school, that would be hard to do.

"That's thoughtful of you," she said, tapping her pen on her leg.

Ryan's eyebrows lifted. "So, you *are* going to bring someone?"

"No." She forced herself to keep a straight face. "But it was nice of you to offer."

His shoulders looked tense, his hand gripping the back of the couch. He opened his mouth to say something but remained silent.

Hailey capped her pen. "Of course, I don't have a boyfriend to bring, but maybe I'll invite my best friend."

"Do you want to see my favorite bug?" Kendra asked, hopping toward her uncle, then leaping on the couch.

"Absolutely." He flicked his gaze to Hailey and back at his niece.

She held two bugs behind her back. "You have to guess."

Ryan's arms relaxed, a smile tugging at his mouth. Hailey caught his eye and shook her head, eyes widening. She'd told him Kendra's favorite bugs already. Hopefully, he'd guess wrong on purpose.

"Hmm. Let me think." He tapped a finger against his chin. "Is it a butterfly?"

Kendra gasped. "Yes. Which one?"

"Monarch?"

"No! It's a blue morpho!" She pulled a blue and black butterfly from her back and he made a dramatic show of losing, smacking his palm against his forehead. Kendra giggled. "What else?"

"Well, I'm going to have to guess dung beetles."

"Ew, Uncle Ryan! Wrong again. It's a praying mantis!" She showed him her large praying mantis hand puppet, and he fell back on the sofa, his hands covering his face. "What's your favorite bug?"

He peeked at her from behind his hands and sat up slowly. "You really want to know?"

She giggled, nodding.

"Well, actually, you've probably heard of it. My favorite bug is a Kenny Beetle!" He took his niece in his arms, tickling her furiously as she laughed, and Ryan grinned. Hailey leaned back, laughing, the glow of humor beaming in her chest. The man had not been around Kendra much in her life, since he lived across the country and never came home to visit, but he was so good with her. He knew the right things to say to make her smile, but more importantly, his interactions with her felt authentic.

Ryan clearly cared for his niece, and that was insanely attractive.

Kendra pulled free and ran to the other side of the room, panting. "No more tickling."

"Okay, fine." Ryan raised his arms in submission.

Kendra knelt back by her toys, a comfortable smile lighting her face. "Are you coming to my concert tomorrow?"

Ryan nodded. "You know I wouldn't miss it. Is your nanny coming, too?"

"Yes. She wouldn't miss it, either," Kendra said, with all the confidence of a girl who knew how much she was loved.

Ryan stood. "Then I look forward to seeing you both there. But now I need to get home. Sergeant is waiting for me."

Sergeant?

Kendra bounced on her cushion. "Can I come? I want to see your Christmas tree."

He screwed up his face into an apology. "Unfortunately, I don't have a tree, so there's nothing to see but my tiny apartment and my overactive dog."

Ah, a dog.

"That's fine with me," Kendra said, her innocence bringing a smile to Hailey's face.

Ryan glanced up at Hailey questioningly. Was he inviting them along with that look? First, he asks if she has a boyfriend, then he invites her over? She shook her head. She had to keep working on her song list for *his* event. "We can't today, unfortunately. Maybe another time."

"Why does Sergeant need you now?" Kendra asked, her little nose scrunching up.

"He needs to go for a walk in the middle of the day, and my neighbor who usually does it for me went out of town for the holidays, so I have to go home and take him out before I can go back to work."

"That sounds like a fun job."

"It probably is. For her," Ryan agreed. "She's a college student so I bet she appreciates the easy money."

Kendra sat up taller. "Can I walk Sergeant next time she goes out of town? I've never done it before, but Hailey can help me."

"Maybe," Ryan said. "I'll have to talk to your nanny about it."

"It probably won't work while you're in school, Ken," Hailey said. "You only get out early today and tomorrow because it's the week of Christmas."

"How long is your neighbor out of town?" Kendra asked her uncle.

He looked amused, his eyes shining. Was he only seeing now how relentless this girl could be when she wanted to be? "She doesn't get back until January. I think she went home until the next semester begins." Ryan tilted his head in a quick motion like he was trying to indicate to Hailey to follow him from the room. He stood. "Bye Kenny. Love you, pipsqueak."

Kendra wrinkled her little nose. "You say weird things." She returned her attention to her bugs.

Ryan took his coat from the back of the sofa, and Hailey set her pad of paper and pen on the side table. "I need to talk to your uncle really fast, Ken. I'll be right back."

Kendra shrugged, maintaining her focus on her plush insects.

Hailey's heart hammered in her chest as she followed Ryan from the room. Attraction bit at her, making her overthink every word she said. She wasn't blind to the fact that he'd just tried to scope out whether she was single or not. But she also knew he was a high-powered magazine exec, formerly a high-powered music exec, and he was way out of her league. Guys like this flirted for fun, and they didn't mean anything by it.

But that didn't make him any less hot. She watched Ryan slip his coat on and button it as she walked through the long, open dining room, kitchen, and into the entryway. "What's up?" she asked, trying to sound breezy. She was pretty sure she'd bypassed breezy and just made her voice sound airy and brainless.

He turned, regarding her seriously, and her gut clenched. "I didn't know if telling you this would be helpful or harmful, but I figured it was better to prepare you."

Hailey crossed her arms over her chest and leaned her shoulder against the wall. Her pulse steadily increased while she watched Ryan layer up to go back into the winter air. Who knew putting *on* so many clothes could be attractive?

She tried to sound light-hearted. "I would usually prefer to be prepared, but now you're just scaring me."

His face broke into a broad smile. "Nothing to be scared of. I know you're aware that when you perform for the party the room will be full of music executives, producers, agents..."

Hailey nodded, trying to swallow against a suddenly sandy throat.

"Well, I got word today that one of the executive producers of Remmy Records will be in town, who happens to be a friend of mine and accepted an invitation to the party. Remmy Records is constantly scouting for new talent. They want to be the first to discover the next big thing."

The floor slipped out from beneath her—or that's how it felt. It was one thing to know she was singing for a group of people who might notice her—she was meant to be, essentially, background noise—but it was entirely different knowing a man was coming with the sole purpose of hearing her.

What would happen if she impressed him?

Her entire life could change.

Ryan dipped his head to make eye contact with her. "I thought you'd be a little more excited than this."

"You should feel my heart," she said. "It's racing."

His lips turned up at the ends, and he took a step closer, holding her gaze and lowering his voice. "This could be huge, Hailey."

"I know. That's why I can't feel my arms right now." She held herself so tightly that she'd cut off the circulation to them, but excitement and anticipation swirled within her, and she couldn't seem to calm her heart or her hold.

"Here." Ryan took her wrists, gently prying them apart. In his hands, she felt like butter melting on toast, immediate warmth shooting up her arms and turning her to liquid. Or maybe that was the blood rushing back into her hands.

"Better?"

Hailey nodded.

"Good." He hadn't released her wrists, and she didn't want him to. Her skin seared where he touched it, her heart fluttering, pattering against her chest like those butterflies Kendra was so obsessed with.

Keeping his voice down, he spoke softly. "Let me know if I can do anything to help you prepare."

"Just stay off YouTube, and don't critique any more of my stuff before I have to go on stage."

Ryan's face fell into a wry smile, but he let go of her hands and took a small step back.

Seriously, Hailey? You had to go and push him away?

"I better go," he said.

"Yeah, thanks for letting me know about the producer."

His lips tipped into a crooked smile. "Sure thing."

Ryan input his code for the elevator and slipped inside, disappearing as the doors closed. Hailey leaned back against the wall, dropping her head back and puffing up her cheeks. Dating was no good while she was chasing a career. Dating was a bad idea. Dating wasn't even possible with a man who was so far up and out of her league—he even called her *your nanny* when talking to Kendra. Kendra knew Hailey's name. She was six, not stupid.

Hailey's phone buzzed in her pocket, and she pulled it out, surprised to find *Amber Martinez* flashing across the screen. Sliding it to answer, she put the phone to her ear.

"Hi, Amber. What can I do for you?"

"Are you and Kendra home?" Her tone was curt, disapproving.

"Yes."

"Was my brother just there?"

Hailey paused, glancing at the white elevator doors. She knew Amber got alerts each time the elevator was used, and everyone in their family, plus Hailey and the cleaning lady, Megan, had their own codes. "Yes, he just left."

"Why was he there?"

Hailey pushed off from the wall, alarm bells going off in her head. "He stopped by on his way home so he could see Kendra."

"Is that all?"

"Well, he gave me some information about the anniversary party, but—"

"Listen, it's great that Ryan set this gig up for you. It was really nice of him, and I'm sure you'll do great. Just trust me when I tell you that he's bad news. I love my brother to death, but you don't want to go there. He left a long, toxic relationship to move back home, and he's not *really* into you, he's just trying to rebound. It's human nature."

"I don't think he's—"

"It's fine. Don't beat yourself up over it. He looks like the perfect package, but there's a lot going on beneath the surface that you just don't want to touch with a ten-foot pole, okay?"

Hailey's stomach dropped. Was she that obvious? Clearly, she had to be, or Amber wouldn't be warning her away. "Yeah. Okay."

Amber sighed. "I have to work extra tonight to make up for ducking out early tomorrow for the concert. And can you remind Megan to get the spare room ready? My mom's flight was moved so she arrives in the morning tomorrow instead of the afternoon."

"Definitely."

"Great. Bye."

The line went dead, and Hailey clicked her phone off, sliding it into her back pocket. She had done nothing but try to ignore the attraction she felt toward Ryan since the moment he threw a sandwich at her. She wasn't doing a great job of it if Amber could tell from her office halfway across Manhattan that Hailey's heart went crazy every time she saw Ryan.

The man was trouble, and it would be wise for her to keep him at a distance.

CHAPTER TEN

The last time Ryan saw his mother she had flown out to LA to watch the Harmony Music Awards with him—his company had scored him a couple seats—and he had introduced her to his girlfriend. That was a year and a half ago, and now he had no girlfriend and no back-to-back music events to distract her from the pathetic turn his life had taken. Standing near the baggage claim at LaGuardia Airport, his hands in his pockets to keep off the chill, Ryan searched the crowd of incomers for his mother. If he had to guess, she was busy somewhere with a mirror making sure her red lipstick was perfect before leaving the terminal.

The crowd milled around Ryan and the baggage terminal that displayed the flight number from Orlando, and he stepped away when his gaze landed on a woman in a dark purple coat, her vivid red hair styled in the short, precise bob she'd worn for the last fifty years. A smile tugged at his lips when he noticed her flawless red lipstick. It was comforting to know that some things never changed.

"Mom," he said, stepping forward to pull her into an embrace.

She gently returned the hug and looked around. "Have you

gotten my bag? I want to go see my grandbaby."

"Not yet. What color is it?"

"Black, hard-side."

Ah. So just like every other piece of luggage coming through LaGuardia right now. "Any colored tags or anything?"

"No."

Well, Ryan just had to hope he'd grab the right suitcase from the luggage carousel. He stood at the head of the rotating belt and was relieved to find that most people had taken their bags and left. A hard-side, black suitcase rolled his way and he leaned forward to pull it from the carousel when a woman's voice spoke just behind him.

"That's mine."

"Oh, sorry—" Ryan gripped the handle and turned, words failing him when he set his eyes on the short, blonde woman with the sleek bob and tan power suit. He hadn't seen her in a month, and while he'd expected to run into her next week at the party, it was weird seeing his ex-girlfriend in the airport. Next to his mother.

"Hey, Jo," he said, pulling her suitcase from the carousel and setting it in front of her. "Did you come in from Florida, too?"

"Yes." She took her suitcase, rolling it closer to her side, her pleasant smile trained on him. "My sister moved out to Orlando a few weeks ago. I went down to help her unpack."

"I had no idea."

"I actually ran into your mom on the flight," Jo said, her pale blue eyes glued to him. If it was up to her, they'd still be together, but Ryan didn't exactly know why. They had been terrible together, and the last year of single life had shown him exactly how little they were meant to be.

Jo was tactful and hadn't made working at the same company a chore. They had stayed friends, at least, as well as could be expected.

"Where in the city are you heading?" he asked. "Can I give

you a ride?"

"Yeah, actually, that would be great." She pulled her purse higher on her shoulder. "I'm staying at my mom's."

Ryan turned back toward the luggage carousel and saw another black suitcase rounding the bend out of sight. He'd have to wait for it to come around again, and he was fine with that. He could hear his mom chatting with Jo behind him, and he needed a moment to think critically. Jo could hand Hailey a career if she wanted to, but she could just as easily stamp out any possibility of Hailey succeeding in the music industry. Jo had a lot of influence, and she knew everyone who was worth knowing.

The trouble was, he didn't know the best way to awe her. Should he show her the video now? Send her the demo? Or wait and let her experience Hailey's live, raw voice in person?

The lone, black suitcase approached again, and Ryan reached for it, lugging the enormous, heavy thing onto the floor. What had his mother packed? Books? He turned, pausing to watch Jo and his mom laughing together.

If there was one thing he knew about Jo that probably hadn't changed, it was her intense jealous streak. The driving force that made her so formidable when facing other record labels was her immense desire to be the best in the business and be the first to discover new talent. But it had also made her a miserable girl-friend. Ryan knew that if she sensed his growing attraction to Hailey, it could become a problem.

Or maybe he was too full of himself and needed to quit worrying about things that probably weren't even an issue anymore. They hadn't even dated for an entire year. They'd been broken up for longer than they'd been together. Maybe he'd been wrong, and she didn't want to get back together.

"Are you ladies ready to go?" Ryan asked, flashing them a smile and taking Jo's suitcase from her. They both turned toward the parking lot, and Ryan moved to lead the way while

KASEY STOCKTON

he caught snippets of their conversation. Orlando's weather, the rude man on the flight who had begged the flight attendant for a seat upgrade, and whether it was worth it or not to brave the cold to see the enormous tree in Rockefeller Center.

Neither of them thought the tree was worth the cold or the crowds.

But Ryan did. He liked the magic of it and the lights, and he didn't mind the ice skating either. Then again, he and Jo hadn't agreed on a lot of things except music. When it came to music they were pretty much in sync.

He hoped, for Hailey's sake, that *that* fact remained the same.

Hailey waited on the sidewalk for the teacher to open the door and let the kids out. It was the final day of school and Christmas vacation was about to begin for Kendra. Until they returned later that evening for the Christmas concert, of course.

Hailey had just the perfect thing in mind to celebrate.

If Amber and Luis chose to keep their house mostly minimalist during the holidays, that was their choice, and she didn't judge them. But Hailey knew there were ways to feel the magic of Christmas without a train around the tree skirt or festive nutcrackers lining the hearth.

And it would start with the biggest tree in New York City.

The front door opened, and the kindergarten teacher stood there, scanning the crowd of waiting parents, grandparents, and nannies. She started sending kids out one at a time to their guardians and eventually made it to Kendra, who hopped down the steps in her tan pants and white polo shirt, covered in a navy sweater and a thick coat. Her cheeks were rosy from the chilly

84

winter air, and her backpack bounced as she walked. "Can we go get hot chocolate at the Corner Bakery?" she asked the moment she reached Hailey, taking her hand.

"No, but I have a feeling you're going to forgive me."

"Why?'"

"Because I have an even better surprise planned."

Kendra grinned all the way to the subway station, guessing every possible treat in Manhattan except for the one they were headed toward. By the time they arrived on the sidewalk outside of Magnolia Bakery, Kendra was stumped. But she took one look at the frosted windows and squealed.

"Cupcakes!"

"Yes!" Hailey clapped her gloved hands together. "Or cheese-cake. Or a cookie. Whatever your little heart fancies."

Kendra threw her little arms around Hailey's waist. They stepped inside the bakery, the warmth wrapping them in the cozy scent of baked goods. Lining up together, they discussed the treats through the glass display case, purchased their cupcakes, and took them back outside.

Hailey turned to her little charge. "Want to go see the big tree?"

"Yes!"

They made their way toward Rockefeller center, finding a bench free of tourists where they could plant themselves while they ate their cupcakes and took in the majesty of the tree.

"Are you excited for your concert tonight?" Hailey asked before taking a bite of her chocolate cupcake.

"Yeah, I guess so."

Well, Kendra definitely didn't have the drive for attention or feed off the thrill of performing like Hailey had as a child. Which was fine. The girl was clearly going to grow up to be an insect scientist. That was probably a thing.

"Did you know my Uncle Ryan doesn't have a Christmas tree? I think that's really sad." Kendra's gaze was fixed on the giant tree in front of them, every square inch covered in lights. It shined better at night, of course, but this felt safer.

Hailey licked the frosting from her thumb. "I did know that. I was there when he told you."

"Why do you think he hasn't gotten a tree?" Her voice lowered. "Do you think he hates Christmas?"

"No, I don't think that. Maybe he doesn't want his dog to chew it up. Or maybe he just hasn't had time to get one. He's probably busy."

"Maybe." Kendra shoved another bite of cupcake in her mouth and slumped back on the bench. "I'm stuffed."

Smiling, Hailey took the remaining half of her cupcake and tossed it back in the box with their wrappers. Her phone started buzzing, and she pulled it out, pausing as she read the name.

Ryan Bierman.

"Hello?" she asked, putting the phone to her ear and trying to sound completely natural.

"Hey, how are you?"

"Cold right now. You?"

He chuckled softly. "Warm. Listen, I'm at Amber's place with my mom, and we were waiting for Kendra. Are you guys on your way home from school? I thought you mentioned yesterday that she got out early today."

"She did." Hailey stood up fast, the box of cupcake remnants and wrappers falling to the cold ground. "Shoot, I had no idea you'd be waiting for us! I thought your mom would be tired after her flight."

"No worries. Any idea when you'll be home?"

"We can come right now. We're just at Rockefeller Center looking at the tree. I'll grab an Uber, so you don't have to wait, and we'll be there—"

"Wait, you're where?"

"Rockefeller Center."

"*Just* to look at the tree?"

There was silence on the phone for a second and Hailey briefly registered Kendra picking up the white Magnolia Bakery box and throwing it in the trash can next to their bench. She reached for the girl's hand, and they started walking toward the street.

Hailey lowered her voice. "Look, I know you don't really care about Christmas trees, but—"

"No, I was just surprised, that's all," Ryan said. "I was talking to someone today about Rockefeller Center...but never mind that. Who said I don't care about trees?" Much to Hailey's surprise, he sounded stung.

"You told me and Kendra you don't have one. And you've never heard of wassail."

"Okay, I think there has been a huge misunderstanding here. I absolutely love Christmas trees. And decorations, and sugar cookies, and all the good parts about the holidays. And not everyone has heard of wassail. I've just been busy preparing for an important meeting and haven't had time yet to decorate."

"And an event and getting your special New Year's edition ready to go to print," she added.

"Exactly."

"Well, I won't take up any more of your time. We're headed your way, and we'll see you soon."

"Great. Thanks. I'll let my mom know."

"Okay. Bye, Ryan."

"Bye, Hailey."

She hung up, swiping on the screen to find her Uber app and request a ride.

"Why are we hurrying?" Kendra asked as they waited on the sidewalk for the car to show up.

"Because there's a surprise waiting for you at the house."

"Better than cupcakes?"

Hailey pictured Ryan in his blue button-down shirt and lazy smile. "Way better than cupcakes."

CHAPTER ELEVEN

Ryan leaned forward on his elbows against the wooden kitchen table and dropped his face in his hands. From the moment Hailey had arrived at the apartment with flushed cheeks, hastily pulling Kendra along, he had been unable to tear his gaze from hers for longer than a few minutes. She'd greeted his mother like an old acquaintance with a kiss on the cheek, and he'd been *jealous* of his mom. For a kiss on the cheek.

So he'd left the room, claiming to need to check in on some things at work and setting up his computer at the dining room table. But the truth was his team had things under control. Half the employees were out of the office due to the holidays, and he still had proofs coming his way constantly, and they all looked great.

Carter was currently on the set of Janica Harper's photoshoot getting the cover all sorted and had texted twice that things were going really well.

Everything was running smoothly.

What Ryan failed to understand, though, was why a team who'd worked so well together the last few weeks had been slowly killing the magazine over the previous few years. If he couldn't pinpoint where it had been failing, how was he going to prevent it from continuing to happen?

He pulled up the numbers sheets again and looked over the updated percentages.

Smooth, velvety laughter drifted from the living room, and Ryan lifted his head to hear it better. Hailey didn't just have the singing voice of an angel. Her voice was purely angelic in every form. Speaking to her earlier on the phone, he had decided he could easily listen to her talk all day. But her laughter? That was a whole different level.

What he really needed to do was just ask the woman on a date. Once Jo was away from Manhattan, of course, and had already offered Hailey a contract.

His phone rang, and he hit the speaker button once he saw that it was Carter. "Hey man, what's up?"

"Any chance you can get down here?"

Why hadn't Ryan knocked on wood? He'd only *just* thought about how well things were going. "What's going on?"

Carter's voice dropped. "Vivi just showed up, and apparently Janica didn't know she was coming. Now Janica's threatening to pull out completely."

Shoot. There had to be a way to smooth this over. "Her publicist didn't tell her?"

"Apparently not," Carter said with a sigh.

"I'm twenty-five minutes out, at least. Can you keep everyone there until I arrive?"

"Sure thing. But hurry."

"You got it." Ryan hung up the phone, shoving all his things back into his bag. He was heading for the living room when Hailey came in, almost ramming into him. They both side-stepped.

"Sorry," she said. "Let me get out of your way. I was just heading out."

"Oh, me too. What about Kendra?"

"She and your mom are going to get ready for the concert together. I have to go home and change."

He nodded, his gaze holding hers. She tucked a dark curl behind her ear, the loose waves falling over her shoulders. Stepping around her, he started toward the stairs, backward. "Don't go anywhere yet."

She gave him a puzzled nod, and he crossed to the stairs, catching his mother and Kendra halfway up them. "Hey Mom, I'm needed at work. I'll meet you both at the concert." He winked at his niece.

"You won't miss it though?" Kendra said, uncertain.

"Of course not. I just need to iron something out really quickly. I'll be there. Don't worry. I wouldn't miss my favorite girl's special night."

She grinned at him, revealing a gap in her teeth that made his heart squeeze.

"Be safe," his mother said, and he shot her a dry smile.

Hurrying back toward the foyer, he found Hailey waiting with her coat and scarf on, pulling gloves over her hands.

She glanced up and caught his eye. "What's going on?"

Punching his code into the elevator, Ryan moved inside and held the door for Hailey to follow him. She stepped close to his side, searching his face.

"Is everything okay?" she asked, her eyes looking concerned.

"I hope so." He hadn't expected her to stand so close or smell so good. He drew in a shallow breath as the doors closed, dimming the small space, and did his best not to look up at the mistletoe hanging over them. What he would give to take advantage of the plant above them right now...but that would have to wait. "I've got a work ruffle I need to smooth over. I was going to ask if you wanted to come."

"To your office?"

He shook his head. "To a studio down in SoHo where my team is right now with Janica Harper."

Hailey's mouth dropped open, her eyes widening. He had to swallow, to focus on keeping his face neutral. Interacting with famous musicians wasn't new to him, and he'd met most of his idols throughout the course of his life—one of the perks of being the son of a major media company that ran a music magazine.

But it had its drawbacks, as well. He'd also been dealt the blow of knowing friends were trying to use him to further their careers in the music industry, or of wondering if girls he met at parties were into him or his name.

That had been one of his issues dating Jo. She'd loved the appearance they made as a successful power couple, how dating drew more attention to them because they were equally successful, and how Ryan's family history had such prominence in the music industry.

He wanted a relationship that uplifted and fulfilled him, not another mutually beneficial business arrangement.

Hailey was different. She was prideful, maybe. She *had* nearly refused to play the gig of a lifetime—for a new artist, at least—simply because she was mad at Ryan, something she'd need to get over if she wanted to succeed in this world. But he knew she wasn't using him just to get further along in her career. If she was, she would've leaped at the chance he gave her to play the party, not practically made him convince her to do it.

Ryan held her excited, widened gaze, a smile pulling at his lips. "Is that a yes?"

"Absolutely. I *loved* her when I was in junior high. Like my entire wall was covered in her posters. I wanted to *be* Janica Harper when I grew up."

Ryan scrunched his face as if considering her differently. "Nah. I'm glad you're Hailey Grant."

She shot him a smile, turning to lean back against the wall, her eyes glazing over. Ryan chuckled, punching in his code again and hitting the button to take them downstairs. Maybe if he stared at the ribbon-wrapped mistletoe above the door, it would draw Hailey's attention there...but he didn't want to be a creep.

She stood up abruptly. "The concert. I was going to change into something nicer."

Sweeping his gaze over her outfit, he thought her dark jeans and short boots were fine. Hadn't she been wearing a plain gray t-shirt under that super puffy coat? "It's an elementary school concert. I think you're fine."

She screwed up her nose. "You don't know these parents if that's your response. It's a fashion show with a children's concert on the side."

The doors opened, and they stepped into the lobby, waving to the doorman on their way outside.

Ryan ordered an Uber and they stood on the sidewalk to wait. "Well, are you going for Kendra, or are you going for the other parents?"

Hailey laughed, nudging Ryan's shoulder with her own. "Unfair. But yeah, okay, you've chastised me. I won't worry about it. I'd way rather go stand in the same room as Janica Harper for a minute than dress up for a bunch of snooty—" She looked at him sharply, her words ending abruptly, and he had to swallow his amusement.

Their Uber car pulled up to the curb, and they slipped onto the backseat.

"I'm glad you got the stain out of your coat." Ryan gestured to the place where his accidentally-propelled greasy sandwich had landed. "I thought I was going to have to replace it."

Hailey put on her seatbelt and pulled her hair to the side. "Yeah, my stain spray saved you this time."

"Thank it for me. So you were pretty familiar with my mom. I didn't realize you knew her."

Hailey nodded. "She's the best. She comes up here a few times a year to spend time with Kendra. That girl has a very doting grandmother."

Interesting. Why didn't he know this about his own family? LA was too far away from the people he loved most, that was for sure. "And you get along with her?"

She looked at him questioningly, and he shrugged. "She just doesn't usually approve of most women I introduce her to."

"Well, there's the difference. You didn't introduce me to her." She grinned. "Besides, she doesn't have to judge whether or not I'm good enough for her son, just her granddaughter."

True, even if he hoped that wasn't the case for too much longer. A blush rose up Ryan's neck, and he pulled out his phone to send a text to Carter to let his friend know how close they were. He had some major schmoozing to do to appease this diva. They were three days away from their deadline. There was no time to set up another shoot, and Sarah had already completed the interview and sent it to him for approval.

"So what can I expect?"

"Honestly?" he asked, shifting on the seat to look into her eyes.

"Yeah..."

"They ran into some trouble. So you can expect an angry musician and a whole lot of flustered *Sound* employees."

"Wait, what?"

The car stopped, and Ryan got out of the car, holding the door open for Hailey. She followed him onto the sidewalk in front of a tall brick building. "It shouldn't be too hard to smooth things over. You ready?"

She nodded, but she looked uncertain. "Yep."

CHAPTER TWELVE

Hailey sat on a chair against the back wall of the loft. Wide, open windows shed natural light over the room. There were people behind a multitude of computers and equipment, all facing the backdrop and lighting equipment. Tables ran along the opposite wall with a coffee machine and water bottles, remnants of lunch sprinkled on platters, and plates of untouched cookies.

Ryan stood near the backdrop speaking to a tall, blond man, Janica Harper, and Vivi Meier. Hailey still couldn't get over the fact that she was seeing both members of the hit girl duo, Cali Girls, in the flesh. *Cali Girls.* They hadn't been seen together amiably in years. Not that either of them looked amiable now.

Hailey stood, pacing toward the food table. Her fifteen-year-old self would've given her right arm to be allowed in the same room as her idols. Now she was in the same room as them, but they were missing the dark eye makeup, knee socks, and grunge shirts that had iconified their look. A look Hailey had desperately—and ineffectually—done her best to imitate in junior high and high school.

Trays of cookies lined the edge of the table and appeared as if they hadn't been touched. Did no one in the music industry eat cookies? These were even shaped like wreaths with big red bows. She took one, watching Ryan try to appease the women—if his hand motions were any indication—and took a bite of the sugar cookie, circling toward the wall of windows until she was close enough to make out some of the conversation.

"I never agreed to this," Janica said with a bite. "So either get her out of here or you can't use any of my images on your cover."

Her images? Like, the ones they had already taken today? Did she own them, or did *Sound Magazine*? Hailey had no idea how all this worked.

The tall blond shared a look with Ryan, and he drew in what appeared to be a steadying breath.

"I should sue," Vivi said, her voice just as high as Hailey remembered it being from interviews. She'd always wondered if that was an affectation, but it sounded real now. "You promised me publicity. I was told I'd have a page inside the mag, and now I show up and have to deal with *this*." She swept her arm toward Janica without a glance, and Janica took a step back, disgust on her face.

Ryan put up an appeasing hand. "We aren't asking you to resolve your differences—"

"Good," Janica spat. "Because that's impossible."

Hailey's heart tugged. The animosity between the two ex-band members was thick, and it was totally killing her holiday cheer. She took a big bite of the wreath cookie to ebb the negativity.

"Exactly." Vivi scoffed. "I would never forgive the woman who stole my boyfriend."

Janica gasped, pivoting toward the redhead. "*Your* boyfriend? You and Brad went on *one* date, and it didn't even end well! You called me after it was over to whine about how obnoxious he was."

"Hearsay."

"It's not hearsay, you lunatic! It's my *memory*! Besides, that doesn't even make sense."

"Let's call it a wrap," someone mumbled behind Hailey. "We can't shoot *this*."

Or...what if they could? She'd heard Ryan say that they only had a few days to finalize the special edition to send to print. What if, instead of shooting a blissfully fake reunion, they shot the real thing? Hailey remembered when the Cali Girls split up because of Brad Donovan, and how it had wrecked her world. She'd hated Brad Donovan, of course, but there were a lot of articles assuming what happened, and nothing from the actual stars themselves. She had always wondered what actually happened. Who *really* had him first. Because after a month, neither of the Cali Girls was with Brad Donovan, but their hatred for each other was strong.

Janica turned on her heel and began stomping away, running her hands through her long, black curls.

But Hailey's wheels were turning, and her idea just might work. What if *Sound* gave these women an opportunity to defend themselves?

"Wait!" Hailey called, and silence fell over the loft, Janica's heels clicking to a stop.

Ryan glanced at her sharply, his eyes widening. She wanted to reassure him, but he wasn't close enough, so she swallowed the nerves that rose in her chest and held Janica's eye. "What if we don't shoot a fake reconciliation?"

Janica rolled her eyes, turning to go again.

"No, hear me out. What if we—"

"Who are you?" someone asked from behind Hailey. "Do you even work here?"

Ryan lifted his hands, staving off the sudden murmuring, and set his gaze on Hailey. "Quiet, team. Let's hear her out."

Hailey shot him a smile. "Janica, Vivi, instead of trying to pretend there's no more anger between you, what if we do a shoot focusing on the split?"

"Why? That was years ago," Vivi asked, derision dripping from her tone. What was *her* beef? She was the one who came here willingly today.

Hailey squared her shoulders, hoping she appeared more confident than she felt. "So you each have a chance to tell your side of the story."

"Janica's interview has already gone to formatting," a short woman said from near the computers.

"That will stay, obviously," Hailey said. "What I'm suggesting is an additional piece. Grab a photo of Janica and Vivi back to back—not touching, obviously—and give them each a chance to speak openly about the split." She narrowed her gaze on Janica, then Vivi, pointing at each of them, her heart hammering. "This gives you both the chance to be raw, real, and open and give closure to yourselves and your fans."

Of which Hailey was one. She was not being selfish in this quest, though. At least, not entirely. While she badly wanted to hear both sides of what had started the feud the women had kept tight-lipped about for the last decade, she knew Ryan needed this, that his magazine desperately needed this.

"I don't know," Janica said. "I'm not sure what I get out of this."

Hailey raised her eyebrows. "A stab at innocence. Are you faultless? Do you believe Brad Donovan was yours for the taking and you *didn't* steal him from your bandmate and best friend? Here's your chance to explain your side of things. You both have moved on with successful careers, but this feud has remained, and no one really knows what happened."

The women looked like they were considering her words, so Hailey kept going. "You want to sell a lot of magazines? Do you want your face plastered all over the internet when this epic exclusive drops? Because it will be. Your fans haven't gone anywhere, and they're dying for something like this."

"This could work," Ryan said, as though coming to the conclusion himself. "Ms. Harper, Ms. Meier, will you give us a chance to tell your story?"

The silence in the room was broken by the beeping of cars outside and the nervous tapping of someone's nails on a phone case in the room somewhere. Vivi looked at Janica, and they held each other's gazes for a moment, neither of them smiling. They seemed capable of understanding one another, though, because they both turned to Hailey at the same time. Vivi nodded, and Janica shrugged.

"Okay, let's do this."

Hailey tried to keep her smile to a professional level, but inside she was absolutely beaming.

Ryan stepped forward. "Wardrobe?"

"Here!" a guy called at the back of the room.

Janica and Vivi started toward the bald guy with the rack of clothes, and Ryan moved to follow them, the tall blond beside him. He stopped, looking at her. "You coming?"

Hailey pointed to her own chest, and Ryan's face broke into a grin. "Yes, *you*. This was your idea. Come on."

She hurried to his side, unable to dampen her smile now.

He leaned in close, whispering. "You were brilliant back there. That was so inspired. And here I thought you were just a nanny."

"A nanny who had a major obsession with Cali Girls back in the day." She leaned in closer. "Their posters are still up on my walls in my childhood bedroom, but don't give me away. I'm trying to keep my cool here."

"Oh, you're definitely doing that."

Ryan's tone of voice gave her pause, and she looked at him sharply, her breath abandoning her lungs. He'd sounded so invested, so meaningful.

"Hey, boss, any preference on the clothes?"

Ryan's focus was stolen by the blond guy, and he looked between the man with the clothing rack and the women they were going to dress.

No one said anything, so Hailey spoke her thoughts. "What about going back to the band's old schtick but modifying it so you each look a little more like the images you've developed now?"

The tall blond guy grinned, pointing at her. "I like this one. She's smart."

"Thanks," Hailey said, but it sounded more like a question.

"Carter," he explained, holding his hand out for her to shake. She shook it, then he turned back to the wardrobe people. "Do we have the stuff for that? Short skirts, knee-high socks. T-shirts, right?"—he turned toward the ex-Cali Girls—"That sort of thing?"

She had to give Carter some props. The guy knew his music history. Or maybe he was a closet fan, too.

The women nodded, and Janica stepped forward, leafing through the wardrobe options until she pulled out a short, houndstooth pleated skirt that screamed the sort of vintage sophistication she was building her brand around. She glanced back at Hailey and lifted the skirt. "Did you guys have this planned from the beginning?"

Hailey swallowed her initial shock over having *Janica Harper* directly address her and shook her head. "I actually just tagged along with a friend today. I'm not officially with the magazine."

"Well," Janica said. "I bet they're glad you showed up."

So was she.

The next two hours sped by as the former Cali Girls got dressed, had their hair and makeup attended to, and posed for photos where they were clearly not reconciled. Hailey's favorite image was the one they let her direct, where the women stood back-to-back, a solid foot of space between them, their bodies and faces relaxed as though they were bored with the whole thing.

"Tell America you're over the drama, so they need to get there, too," she had said, and she felt like both women understood her. Maybe they weren't reconciled, but they were tired of it being publicized. It must be insanely annoying to have their private dispute so heavily theorized over and discussed among people who didn't even know them.

The team began wrapping things up, breaking down the equipment and cleaning up their makeup stations. Hailey had eaten three more wreath cookies and stood against the back wall with a water bottle, watching the crew take down the lighting system and backdrops.

If she did well enough at the anniversary party and someone noticed her, this could be her future. Photoshoots, the public knowing everything about her, disputes with her friends that made headlines.

Okay, well, probably not that last one. She would forever be a solo act. But was all this in her future? More importantly, did she want it to be?

"You ready?" Ryan asked, sidling up beside her. He waved to Carter and the blond left with Vivi and her bodyguards out the back door.

Hailey pushed up from the wall. "Sure thing."

He reached for her hand, stalling her. "Hey, you okay?"

"Yeah, definitely. I was just thinking about fame and what it can do to a person."

Ryan held her fingers, pressing them lightly and sending a flurry of warmth over her skin. "Thinking about your career?"

Hailey's cheeks warmed. "Not really. I mean, I know I'll never get this famous, but I was just thinking about the possibilities and how I would react, how it would feel to be in their shoes."

"That's not a bad thing to do. It's important to be realistic about the sort of life you'll lead once Joe offers you a contract."

She grinned. "You say that like it's a done deal."

Ryan's dark eyebrows lifted. "Maybe I think it is."

"You have a lot of confidence in me for someone I've just met."

He shrugged. "I know talent when I see it. That's why I was offered a job at Remmy Records in the first place, and how I got to know Joe."

Hailey thought of everything she knew about Ryan. He'd gotten his start working for *Sound Magazine* while his father had been alive, worked his way up in the company, got famous for his critiques on YouTube for the magazine, then left it all to move to LA and work for Remmy Records. And now he was back.

"Why did you leave it, then? What brought you back to New York?" She held her breath, wishing the answer didn't matter so much. But Amber had said he left a woman and a toxic relationship. What would Ryan say?

His eyes grew serious, fixing on her, and his mouth turned up in a crooked smile. He still held her hand, and she said nothing, afraid he'd release it if she did. "Will I sound completely lame if I say it was because I wasn't happy out there?"

"Not lame," Hailey said. It made him sound sad.

"Just pitiful, I know. What really happened is that Bierman Media's biggest ad account threatened not to renew with us, and the magazine flagged. My dad had his hand in a lot of business ventures, but *Sound* was his baby. I couldn't let it die without doing my best to revive it."

"And hope to find some sort of meaning in the process?" Hailey asked gently.

He nodded, his gaze locked on hers, his hand tightening. "I went away, did my own thing, and now I'm back. New York is my home, and I'm just looking...I guess I'm looking for some contentment now."

Hailey wanted to pull him into a hug, to help him see how valid and worthy that goal was. But she felt locked in place, frozen. It wasn't her place.

He chuckled, breaking the spell. "But we don't have to go over that now. We need to rush over to the school."

"Oh, the concert!" Hailey pulled her hand from Ryan's, taking her phone from her pocket to check the time. "We need to run."

"Then let's run."

CHAPTER THIRTEEN

Ryan got to the office early the next morning and pulled out the prints Tommy had left on his desk the night before. The shots of Janica before Vivi had arrived at the shoot were great, and a few of them would make excellent covers. But the shots after Hailey had intercepted, where Janica and Vivi posed together, but completely apart, were amazing. They were perfect, and music fans were absolutely going to eat this up.

It was a shame they wouldn't have the sales numbers from this edition of the magazine before their meeting with Bradshaw. The issue's success would undoubtedly help matters.

As it stood though, Ryan was still gaining confidence by the minute. His YouTube critique was steadily increasing in views, reviving his old channel in the process and funneling people to articles on *Sound*'s website. Teasers were set to go live on the website tomorrow about the upcoming special edition and the Cali Girls reunion. It was total clickbait, of course, but it would work.

Ryan had a feeling people were going to like what the women had to say. Each of them had told the story from their perspective for the first time ever. It was strange Janica's publicist hadn't warned her about the concept for the shoot, but the woman had been absent yesterday. She must have thought it was a good idea too but had known Janica would never attend the shoot if she'd been forewarned.

It was good for everyone to get this out into the world. Then maybe the women could move on.

Carter poked his head through the doorway. "You're here early."

Ryan leaned back in his chair. "Just wanted to get a pulse on what's already finished, and what still needs sorting for this edition."

Carter nodded, leaning against the door and crossing his arms over his chest. "I was here pretty late with Tommy and Sarah last night, and I think we're nearly ready. Formatting should have everything to you by the end of the day tomorrow if I have my guess."

"Perfect, because Christmas Eve is two days away, so we have no time to lose here."

"Don't worry, man. It'll all go smoothly. You'll be able to check everything off by tomorrow night, I'm sure."

"Let's hope so."

A sly grin slipped over Carter's face. "So, you gonna tell me what's going on with that woman now?"

"Once you tell me how things are going with Sarah."

"Nonexistent, as it should be," Carter said. "Your turn. What's up with the woman from the YouTube video?"

"Who?" Ryan asked, but he knew what Carter was asking. He hoped he looked innocent.

Carter flattened his lips. "You know who. Super pretty. Long, dark hair. Killer smile."

Ryan's throat constricted, a sense of protectiveness falling over him. But Carter was looking at him really closely, so he refrained from telling the guy to back off.

Carter nodded appreciatively. "She clearly has a head for this stuff and not just musical talent. She kind of seems like the complete package."

Ryan thought the same thing. She was exactly who any producer would be thrilled to work with. And he was about to parade her in front of a room full of them.

"She is really talented, but she still has humility. I heard her singing the other day for my niece, and her voice is just so pure and so unique. Man, I really don't think she realizes how good she is."

Carter nodded thoughtfully. "Hopefully LA doesn't squeeze that out of her."

Ryan startled. "What do you mean?"

"Didn't you invite Jo Swenson to come hear her sing?"

"Yeah." He'd told Carter about running into his ex at the airport, too, and how he hoped she would be Hailey's ticket into the music industry. "But I don't see what that has to do with anything."

"If Hailey signs with Remmy Records, she'll have to move to LA."

Ryan felt like Carter had just taken the clock off his desk and chucked it at his chest. The guy was right. There was no way Jo would offer Hailey a contract and allow her to remain on the east coast. She'd be needed in LA nonstop for the next year at least, maybe even longer. It was inordinately unfair that the perfect woman seemed to drop in his lap the moment he got to Manhattan, only to be headed toward a life in LA.

But he wasn't about to do anything to jeopardize her future.

"Good job with the shoot yesterday, though," Carter said, moving on as if he hadn't just dropped a major bomb on Ryan— a bomb he *totally* should have seen coming. "You saved it, man."

Ryan nodded. *He* hadn't really done anything. The real star had been Hailey. She had known exactly what they needed, and she'd killed it. She was going to do really well when she hit the music world, and Ryan couldn't wait to witness the whole thing.

Even if he had to do so from New York.

Ryan watched his friend leave then returned his attention to the photos on his desk. He had to give notes on which ones to use for which pages, but his brain wouldn't focus on the task. It was too busy thinking of Hailey in the open brick loft yesterday and how commanding and intuitive she'd been.

He pulled out his phone and sent her a message.

Ryan: *The photos turned out amazing.*

Hailey: *Wow! That was super fast. Can I get a sneak peek?*

Ryan: *Hang on, let me just send you a non-disclosure agreement first.*

He leaned back in his chair, chuckling to himself. Then he sent another text.

Ryan: *Just kidding. I trust you.*

He spread the images over his desk and snapped a photo, then sent it to her.

Hailey: *Those are even better than I imagined. I'd watch your website when it launches. The sheer volume of fans dying for this information could crash it.*

Well, that was a valid point. He made a note to check with IT and make sure they were equipped to handle an overload of traffic. Hailey's video and the speed it had gained traction was proof that things on the internet could go from zero to a hundred with the snap of a finger.

Ryan: *Good point. So, what are you and Kenny up to today?*

Hailey: *Kendra is spending the day with your mom, so I'm working on my song list.*

Ryan: *How's it coming along?*

Hailey: *Better than I imagined. Thanks for taking me yesterday. That was a once in a lifetime experience.*

Ryan: *Or was it? For all you know, that was just the beginning.*

He watched his phone for the little dots to indicate that she was typing, but nothing happened. He put his phone down after a minute, dropping his head back and closing his eyes. *Why could he not stop thinking about this girl?*

Hailey strummed the guitar listlessly, unable to focus on the lyrics pulled up on her laptop in front of her. She sunk back against the pillows and rubbed her eyes.

"Do you want some lunch?" Nikki called from the kitchen. "I'm trying a new recipe."

"Yes," Hailey called back. "Always." She flipped her phone over but there were no new messages. Not that she expected any. She hadn't texted Ryan back last. His confidence in her was both terrifying and exciting. He legitimately thought she could do this.

Sitting up, she strummed the chords again and hummed the tune of *All I Want for Christmas is You,* before trying out different versions. A cappella, minor, upbeat...they all sounded good. But she needed to try non-Christmas music. By New Year's Eve, she should be playing regular music. She just wasn't ready for that yet. Now, a few days before Christmas, holiday songs were all she wanted to play.

Nikki knocked on the door, holding two plates. "I've got creamy pesto pasta with sun-dried tomatoes and mozzarella chunks."

Hailey scrunched up her nose. "So that smells divine, but 'chunks' sounds gross."

"Yeah, maybe I should rephrase that part when I pitch this to Chef." She sat on the end of Hailey's bed, handing her a plate before scooting back to rest against the wall.

Hailey spun her fork on the spaghetti noodles and took a bite, her mouth watering around the rich basil and garlic sauce. "Wow, Nikki. That is *good.*"

Nikki beamed. "I'll add it to my repertoire."

"Please do." Hailey took another bite. "I could eat this again and again."

"You might have to," Nikki said. "I made way too much."

Hailey speared a mozzarella chunk. "What inspired you to make it?"

"Christmas. You know...green sauce, red sun-dried tomatoes." She gasped. "You know what would make it even better? *Pine* nuts!"

"Pine nuts?"

"Yes!" Nikki jumped off the bed, jostling the mattress, and Hailey had to lean forward to stop her guitar from falling on the floor. "I have to run to the store. Don't take another bite!"

Hailey paused her fork just before it reached her mouth. The scent hit her nose, and she glanced to the doorway, catching sight of Nikki pulling on her coat before the door opened and shut behind her. Hailey ate another bite. She was okay with having a second helping when Nikki returned and added the pine nuts. She was constantly messing with her recipes—this wouldn't be the last time.

Hailey's phone buzzed, and she scrambled to look for it, her heart jumping. Disappointment shot through her when she saw Nikki's name. She'd foolishly hoped it would be Ryan again.

Nikki: *Don't eat!! I know you won't be hungry for seconds if you do.*

Hailey: *I promise you I will try this dish with pine nuts.*

Nikki: *That was not a promise. DON'T EAT!*

Hailey took another bite. The pasta was way too good to stop eating. Regardless of Nikki's funny Christmas inspiration, this dish would be good any time of year. When Hailey thought of the holidays, she thought of Christmas trees, wassail scenting the air, and music—always lots of music. Whether her siblings were playing carols on the piano or her mom was running the local holiday station on her countertop radio, Christmas music was going on in her house all season long as Hailey grew up.

Nikki was to Hallmark movies what Hailey was to classic, overplayed Christmas songs. She could not get enough.

Her phone buzzed. Kendra had sent her a photo from her iPad.

Kendra: *Look what I painted!*

Attached was a photo of a large Christmas tree with a fireplace and stockings. A family was painted beside it, with five adults and a little girl. Judging by the hair colors, Kendra had included her parents, grandma, Uncle Ryan, and Hailey in the portrait, and Hailey's heart squeezed.

Hailey: *Are you painting with Grandma today? I love it!*

Kendra: *Yes and I have a surprise for you, too. See you tomorrow!*

Hailey: *See you girlie! Xoxo*

The image was the perfect Christmas scene. Was that what their holiday would look like?

Her phone started ringing, flashing Ryan's name over the screen, and she jumped, dropping the empty plate on her bed. Quickly sitting up tall and clearing her throat, Hailey moved the plate to her dresser and answered the phone.

"Hey, what's up?"

"I have a major favor to ask of you."

"Yeah?"

His voice went apologetic. "You said you owed me, and I never actually intended on cashing in on that, but I'm just swamped at the office with this edition due, and my dog really needs a walk in the middle of the day. He's still adjusting to life in New York, and—"

"Say no more. I've got you covered." She moved to her closet and pulled out her shoes, tucking the phone between her ear and shoulder so she could put them on.

"You're a lifesaver, Hailey. Seriously, I owe *you* now."

"Actually, I think this makes us even." She moved the phone to her other shoulder and tied her laces. "What do I need to know?"

"He's a big, playful dog. Leash should be next to the door on a hook, and there's a jar of dog treats on the counter. One of those will get him to chill long enough to snap the leash on. Doggie bags are on the handle, so you should be good to go."

"Got it. And a house key?"

"Oh, I've got a keypad. I'll text you the number."

"Should I sign a non-disclosure agreement first?"

He was silent for a second, but then his apologetic voice rang in her ear, soft and husky and causing shivers to run down her shoulders. "That was a bad joke, I know. I have a case of the dad jokes now. Imagine how much worse it'll become when I'm actually one of those."

"Horrifying."

He chuckled. "Yeah, well, I'm just in the office so feel free to call me if you run into any issues, but Sergeant is a good dog and very obedient."

"Okay, you've got it."

"Thanks, Hailey. I wouldn't have asked you to do this if I wasn't desperate." He lowered his voice. "I debated asking my secretary for like twenty minutes but she's not exactly young anymore, and I worry that Sergeant would be too much for her."

"No stress, Ryan. Seriously. It's fine."

"Okay." Was he dragging out the conversation intentionally? It really seemed like he had nothing more to say, but he wasn't getting off the phone. "I'll let you know when I get there—"

"Oh, the address," he said. "I'll text you that, too. If you want to take a cab or an Uber just send me the cost and I'm happy to reimburse you."

"I'm fine with the subway. I've got nothing going on today, so it was good timing."

"You're a saint."

"Well, if that's all…"

"Yeah," he said. "I think that's everything."

"Okay, then I'll talk to you later. Bye, Ryan."

"Bye."

She hung up the phone and stared at it. Why had he been so weird? Like he wanted to say more but didn't. Maybe if she called him after she walked his dog she could get more information then.

Texts came in one after the other with Ryan's address—not too far away via subway, actually—his door code, and a "thank you" GIF.

She grabbed her coat and purse and let herself out.

CHAPTER FOURTEEN

Sergeant wasn't overly huge or anything, but *wow* he was strong. He pulled Hailey along the sidewalk, zigzagging to sniff at undesirable corners or suspicious-looking spots on the sidewalk until they'd nearly circled the block. Catching the street sign on the other corner of the crosswalk, Hailey paused, pulling hard on Sergeant's leash to keep him close. She hadn't realized how close she was to Target, but the moment it occurred to her that the store was an easy walk away, an idea fell into her mind so perfect and so exciting, she started moving that direction almost unintentionally.

Ryan's apartment was a typical minimalist's bachelor pad. The bookshelf had a dozen or so books stacked to one side, with a few random trinkets here or there, and what looked like a framed photo of Ryan and Amber as children, their parents posing behind them.

There was a large dog bed beside the couch and a basket of toys in the corner, but the rest had looked so empty and dismal, it had made her sad for Ryan. Even if he wasn't home much, he deserved something festive and warm to return home to. Or maybe that was Nikki's influence in the back of her mind screaming that everyone needed a little holiday cheer.

If Hailey could pull this off before Ryan got home from work, he'd undoubtedly get his holiday cheer.

She spent the next forty-five minutes walking the aisles at Target and loading her cart up with the essentials: small pre-lit tree and bulb ornaments, a length of garland, twinkling star tree topper, oranges, cinnamon sticks, apple juice, and some holiday shortbread cookies in a blue tin. She went down the stocking aisle on an impulse and chose two—one with a huge, plaid R and the second one with a dog bone.

Directing Sergeant back home with her arms loaded up with more bags than she had strength for was harder than she'd imagined it would be. She just barely managed, only getting Sargeant's leash tangled around her legs once.

The moment Hailey got back to Ryan's apartment, she put everything down, found a pot to boil the wassail in, and got to work.

She commanded the Amazon Echo on his counter to play Christmas music and helped herself to his kitchen, slicing the orange and dropping cinnamon and cloves into the pot before dumping the apple juice. Wassail was a cinch to make, and a slow simmer made the house smell better than a dozen candles could manage.

It smelled like Christmas.

It only took another thirty minutes to make the place look like Christmas too. She set up the small Christmas tree and plugged it in, then hung the garland and twinkle lights over the drapes and bookshelf. The stockings proved the most difficult, but she managed to hang them temporarily from the garland.

Stepping back to survey her work, Hailey couldn't help the smile that spread over her face. This was much better than the empty apartment it had been before, and she had done nothing that Ryan couldn't immediately reverse if he decided he hated it

—except for permeating the apartment with the tangy apple cider, of course, but that would go away with time, and she'd left Ryan's bedroom door closed, something she assumed he did to keep Sergeant away from his shoes.

Now she just needed to write him a note to explain her little surprise, and maybe set some cookies out, and—

A knock at the door broke through her plans and Hailey froze, Sergeant's barking at the door shaking her. It couldn't be Ryan already, right? She glanced at the clock on the microwave and it read six o'clock. Okay, so it *could* be Ryan, but...no, he wouldn't knock on his own door.

And he certainly wouldn't expect her to answer it for him.

Unless it was a package. If he'd had something delivered, she should definitely bring it in. People stole things from in front of doors all the time in her building. Ryan's building was nicer, but people were people. Putting down the cookie tin, Hailey took hold of Sergeant's collar to keep him from bolting and opened the door...to find a short, blonde woman with striking blue eyes wearing a little red dress. Sergeant barked louder, directly at the woman, and Hailey pulled on his collar to keep him from leaping.

"Shh, Sergeant. Hush." She looked up at the woman. "I'm so sorry! I don't know why he's doing this."

The woman gave a curt smile, clearly struggling to mask her surprise. "I didn't know...I mean, I just dropped by—" She cleared her throat, staring frankly at Hailey.

"Ryan isn't here," Hailey said apologetically, tugging on a struggling Sergeant.

The woman didn't look pleased, and Hailey knew a moment's panic. What if Ryan was into this woman, but she made a wrong assumption about Hailey and he lost his chance with her? The idea of that scenario sent a volley of nausea through her stomach.

"I'm just here to walk the dog," Hailey said. "Want me to

leave him a message?"

"No," the woman said quickly, shaking her head. She turned to go.

"Can I get your name?" Hailey called, trying to salvage the situation. "I can let Ryan know you stopped by."

"I'll just call him later. It's not urgent." She left, her stilettos clicking down the hallway. Hailey shut the door and released Sergeant, who jumped on her before turning to run down the hall and back. That poor dog needed more exercise. Hailey was half-tempted to offer to take Sergeant home with her on Christmas Eve to her parents' house, but he wouldn't be fun to handle on the train up to Connecticut, and the offer would probably only make Ryan think that she considered him a bad owner.

Which, she didn't. Any man who had more dog paraphernalia in his living room than things belonging to a human clearly cared about his dog.

Her phone buzzed, and she read the text from her mom.

Mom: *What time does your train get in tomorrow?*

Hailey: *Super, super late. I was planning to let myself in and see you in the morning.*

Mom: *We need to pick you up from the station.*

Hailey: *I'll just grab an Uber.*

Mom: *I don't know about that. That seems very unsafe.*

She chuckled. She lived in New York City, for heaven's sake.

Hailey: *Don't worry. I'll carry my mace in my hand and check the door for the child's lock before I get in the car.*

Mom: *You'll tell me when you get here?*

The time stamp on her phone caught her eye and she froze. What was she doing here still? Ryan could be home any minute. She needed to go.

Hailey: *Yes!*

Nervousness washed over her, and she went for her purse, grabbing it and gathering the trash in a bag to take out with her. She collected all the boxes and stood in the living room, glancing around. Sergeant could easily tear them up, and if Ryan just wanted her to return everything, she should keep them. His bedroom door stood opposite her, untouched, but the idea of Ryan walking in and finding her in there was too much.

Hailey hurried into the kitchen, stacking all the broken-down boxes on top of the fridge when the keypad beeped, and the front door opened. She spun, her cheeks going hot as her eyes caught Ryan's surprised ones.

"What's..." His mouth hung open and he turned, taking in all the changes Hailey had made to his apartment. To *his* home.

Oh, no. The look of pure and utter shock he wore was not the happy, cheerful face she expected.

Her impulse suddenly seemed a lot less sweet and a whole lot more invasive. She didn't know this guy. She knew his sister and his niece, and she kind of knew his brother-in-law, but she didn't know Ryan. She only felt like she did. Him telling her about all he wanted from his life had given her the false impression that she had a right to go and do something about it. But she had merely been a listening ear, and now she had invaded where she had not been invited.

"I'm so sorry. I thought it would be a nice surprise, but I can see how I've misread the situation and overstepped."

"No, you haven't." He put a hand out and absently rubbed Sergeant's head, his gaze tripping over each part of the apartment before landing on Hailey in the kitchen. "What's the smell?"

She swallowed, leaning back against the counter. "Wassail."

His mouth ticked up in a smile. "I should have known."

"Listen," she said, lowering her voice. He had a seriousness about his face that was setting her further on edge. "I can take everything down in like ten minutes, box it up, and get it out of here. You can disappear and come back in and everything will be like it was." She screwed her face up in apology. "Except the smell."

His face broke into a smile, and he pulled his messenger bag from his shoulder, setting it down on the floor against the wall. Ryan kept his gaze on her while he walked around the island into the kitchen and stopped just before her. "I love it."

Her heart galloped in her chest, pounding in her ears. "You do?"

He nodded. "What made you do it?"

"I wanted to thank you for taking me to that photoshoot, for pushing me to perform at the event when I was being stubborn and didn't want to accept anything from you. For asking your friend from Remmy Records to come listen to me. You don't know me, but you've done nothing except help me try to break into the music world since we've met, which I've been diligently trying to do for four years without making *any* progress."

"You've probably honed your performance skills singing at all those bars. So at least that time wasn't useless."

"That's a good point." She smiled at him, his clear hazel eyes trained steadily on her. "You really don't hate your apartment? I can leave so you can rearrange everything to your own taste."

He didn't take his eyes from her. "I love it."

I Saw Mommy Kissing Santa Claus came through the speaker and Hailey's eyes dropped to Ryan's lips. She tore her gaze away, training it on the dog resting at the base of the tiny tree. "Oh, I forgot one last thing."

"Yeah?" he asked, his voice husky.

Hailey stepped past him, reaching into the last Target bag to pull out a small Santa hat with a paw print on the front.

Ryan's eyebrows rose. "Is that for me?"

"No." She stepped further away from him. The space was doing her good, unfogging her brain. "It's for Sergeant."

"Good luck getting him to wear it."

Hailey accepted the challenge. She got down on one knee, clicking her tongue. "C'mere, Sergeant. There's a good boy."

The dog's ears perked up, and he lifted his head before trotting toward her, head slightly bent. She rubbed his ears. "I'm going to give you a cool hat, okay?" Sergeant didn't seem to hear her; his eyes were closing blissfully as she scratched behind his ear until she seamlessly slipped the hat over his head and he froze, looking at her, then Ryan. He barked once, then nuzzled his head against her chest, and Hailey laughed, reaching to scratch him under the belly.

"I win," she said, beaming up at Ryan.

Ryan's expression made her pause, his face serious and warm. Hailey chuckled awkwardly, rising and dusting her hands together. "Well, I better get going."

"Do you have somewhere to be? I was thinking of ordering in, maybe watching a Christmas movie."

"Oh, that sounds..." The blonde that knocked on the door earlier flashed in her mind, followed by Amber's warning that Ryan was dealing with a terrible breakup. Maybe he just wanted a rebound, and maybe hanging out wouldn't kill either of them. "Someone stopped by earlier tonight. I didn't get her name, but she seemed uncomfortable finding me here. I tried to reassure her that I wasn't—that *we* aren't..." She smiled awkwardly.

Ryan's eyebrows drew together. "I wasn't expecting anyone."

"She was short, blonde..." *Insanely gorgeous.* Hailey pulled her purse from the counter and smiled. "Maybe another time. I really need to work on my music for the party."

"Will I see you before Christmas?"

"I don't think so." She crossed to the door, trying to make her voice sound light to cover her disappointment. She *could* stay. She was choosing not to. "I'm heading up to Connecticut for a few days, but I hope you have a great Christmas."

Ryan followed her over to the door, leaning against the wall beside her while she bent over to put her shoes on. When she stood up, she was close to him, closer than she meant to be.

"I will," he said, confident, his eyes sparkling. "This place doesn't feel so sterile anymore, so thanks for that."

"You know, photographs can help with that, too. Or just any sort of personalization."

"I've got a picture up," he defended.

She grinned. "I saw it. You were a cute kid."

Ryan's boyish smile melted her heart. She wanted to reach forward and brush her knuckles over his stubbled jaw, but that would be weird. He would absolutely think she'd gone crazy. Still, her fingers itched by her sides so she clenched her hands, slipping them behind her back.

"Have a good Christmas."

"Thanks," Ryan said. "Same to you."

His arms came around her before she realized what was happening, and her body melted against his, her hands softening their grips. She returned his hug, sliding her arms around his shoulders. His stubble scratched her forehead and she inhaled—trying to do so quietly so he wouldn't notice.

She loosened her hold and he seemed to hesitate a moment before he released her and stepped back, rubbing the back of his neck.

"Bye, Ryan." She turned and walked away, gripping the purse strap over her shoulder as if it would actually infuse her with the strength to keep walking. The guy was hot, insanely powerful, wealthy, thoughtful, kind. He was the entire package.

But he had baggage. He was Amber's brother, and she wouldn't have warned Hailey away if she hadn't had a good reason.

Hailey walked to the subway station telling herself over and over again that she'd made the right choice in leaving his apartment. And now she had a few days free of the Martinez-Bierman clan in order to clear her head.

But if she needed to clear her head...then why did it feel so clear already? Why did she feel like leaving him had been the wrong choice?

CHAPTER FIFTEEN

Ryan sat on the floor of his niece's room as she lined up the new plastic bugs Hailey had given her for Christmas and proceeded to explain what was interesting about each one. He tried to appear interested, but it was hard. Learning that orchid mantises could turn pink and blend in with orchids in Asia was not Ryan's idea of fascinating, but he knew it mattered to Kendra, so he kept his focus on her, engaged.

She picked up a plastic ant as long as her hand. Could her nanny have found bigger bugs? These ones were huge. "Hailey said she'd take me to the zoo when she gets back from her parents' house to see the leaf cutter ants."

"If you want to see ants I bet we could find some right now. We just need to search out the trash cans on the sidewalk."

Kendra laughed. "You're silly, Uncle Ryan." She shifted her attention back to the large, plastic insects lined up on the floor. "What's your favorite bug?"

"You." He leaped for Kendra and tickled her as she giggled.

She wiggled free, running to her bed and hopping onto it. "You always say that!"

A knock at the door took their attention and Ryan's mother

stepped into the room, not a hair out of place in her flawless, red bob, and not a speck of lint visible on her navy jacket.

"What's going on in here?" she asked, stepping inside and sitting on the bed beside Kendra.

"I'm learning all sorts of interesting things about bugs," Ryan said, reclaiming his seat on the floor and leaning against the wall.

"Did you know, Grandma, that the orchid mantis will actually change its color to mimic an orchid? It can blend in with flowers in Asia. I have it in a book if you want to see."

"Oh, I would love it if you read to me."

Kendra screwed up her tiny face. "I can't really read the big words yet, but Hailey has read it to me so many times I memorized it."

"That's kind of her."

Kendra nodded, jumping down to search her bookshelf. "Hailey is really good at reading."

Ryan's mother shot him an amused smile.

"Do you miss Hailey when she isn't here?" his mother asked.

Kendra pulled a book from the shelf and skipped back to her bed. "Yes. She went to see her mom and dad for Christmas and won't come back for three more days. But it's okay because *we* get to spend time together." She threw her arms around her grandmother.

"Would you like to call her now and wish her a merry Christmas?" Ryan asked before he could think better of it.

Kendra brightened. "Yes!"

He pulled out his phone, avoiding his mother's shrewd gaze, and gestured to his lap. Starting a video call to Hailey, he put the phone up to frame Kendra, his heart beating rapidly in his chest.

The phone quit ringing, and it took a moment to connect before Hailey's face appeared on the screen, a wide smile on her lips. "Merry Christmas, Kenny!" she said, grinning.

"Merry Christmas, Hailey! Did Santa bring you anything?"

"He did, but I want to hear about you. How has your day been?"

"Really good. I've been setting up my bugs in a zoo and putting them in families. When you get back we can play with my zoo and then we can go to the *real* zoo."

Hailey grinned, her eyes sparkling. "That sounds perfect, and I absolutely can't wait." She pulled her phone further away, showing an open, brightly lit farmhouse full of people. A plump Christmas tree sat in the corner, gold and red interspersing the greenery hanging over the mantel and wrapping the banister in the background. It was a Christmas haven, strewn with cheer and smiles. "Do you want to say hello to my family, Ken? We're about to start dinner."

"Yes!" Kendra waved, and Hailey turned the camera around so everyone in her parents' house could wave back. The little girl was bouncing on Ryan's knees, she was so happy, and the weight hit him like a solid wall. He had given this girl's nanny a ticket out of her life.

"I miss you," Hailey said, and the crazy part was that Ryan believed her. She stepped out through a door, shifting the camera to show her face again. She genuinely missed this little girl, and it only made him feel worse for inviting Jo out to listen to Hailey.

But, no. He would *not* feel bad about handing Hailey the opportunity to chase her dreams.

"Grandma told me we could make cookies tomorrow. I'll save some for you."

Ryan couldn't imagine his mother making cookies, but he glanced at her and she just smiled.

Hailey laughed. "That is really thoughtful, Kendra. I'm sure you and your grandma are going to have a great time over the next few days."

Kendra nodded. "We will."

Amber's voice carried from downstairs, letting them know it

was time for dinner. Ryan shifted the phone so he could see her, and her smile widened. "Hey," he said. "We have to go eat, too."

"Okay, thanks for calling. It was nice to see your face, Ken."

"You're welcome," Kendra said.

Ryan wanted to stay on longer, to ask how her trip had been and if she was getting nervous for her upcoming performance, but Kendra stayed on his lap and his mother sat watching him. "I hope you have a great Christmas, Hailey."

"Thanks, Ryan. Hey, how's your tree holding up?"

"Good so far. I thought Sergeant would tear it up during the night, but he's left it alone."

"I'm so proud of him." Someone called her name, and she turned her head, nodding. "I have to go. Merry Christmas!"

"Merry Christmas," Kendra and Ryan chorused back, then hung up the phone. The room became too quiet, and Ryan couldn't meet his mother's eye. He helped Kendra stand and got up to follow her downstairs where his sister was pulling a casserole dish from the oven and peeking under the foil.

"We got to talk to Hailey," Kendra said, skipping past her mom to look at the cake on the counter.

Amber glanced sharply at Ryan, and he gave her a smile, moving around the island to take the stack of plates to the table. He could see she wanted to make a snarky remark, so he got out of there before she could. What did it matter if he liked Hailey? It couldn't go anywhere unless she bombed the performance Friday, and he knew that wouldn't happen.

She was too talented not to get noticed.

126

"Who was that?" Sophie asked, waddling across the back deck to sit on the porch swing, tearing off pieces of a dinner roll as she went and popping them in her mouth.

Hailey sat beside her pregnant little sister, using her toes to rock the swing. "Just Kendra. You were in there when everyone waved, right?"

Sophie didn't look fooled. "Yeah. But you already know I was asking about the *guy* on the phone."

"Oh, him?" Hailey smiled, dropping her head back and pushing the swing harder. "Just Kendra's uncle."

"Kendra's *hot* uncle, you mean?"

Hailey's cheeks flushed. "I mean, yeah…he's not ugly."

"And he's comfortable enough with you to video chat?"

"Well, he called for Kendra."

"Mmhmm," Sophie said, her voice disbelieving. She rested a hand on her round belly, her face trained on her sister. "What are you not telling me?"

Hailey shrugged. "I don't really think there's anything to tell. I like the guy, but he's so far out of my league it's not even funny. He went from being a high-powered music exec in LA to the editor-in-chief of New York's biggest music magazine. He's not just successful in his own right, either. His dad was huge in the media industry, and they come from really old New York money."

"It kind of sounds like you're discounting a relationship before even giving yourself a chance to see where it goes. What if he isn't as big of a snob as you are?"

Hailey tucked her chin, scoffing. "I'm not a snob."

"Really? Because you totally sounded like one just now. You won't date the guy because he has a lot of money? Pretty lame excuse."

"*No.* I won't date the guy because he hasn't asked me on a date." Except, he'd invited her to stay for dinner and a Christmas movie the night she set up his apartment. But that hadn't been a date. It had been a thank you. "His sister warned me away from him because he recently got out of a toxic relationship. Not to mention the fact that he just barely moved back to New York, and if he's right and Remmy Records sees a future with me, I'll be moving across the country."

"Excuses." Sophie's hands absently rubbed her belly. "So he's the one that set you up with the party gig next week? I already like him for thinking Remmy Records will see a future with you."

"I'm afraid his confidence is rubbing off on me. He's convinced I'm the next big thing, and he's only heard me sing once. Well…twice, plus he's heard my demo. But what if he's totally wrong and it comes to nothing? My expectations are set so high. I'm going to be so disappointed."

"Don't stress yourself out before you need to. The party is New Year's Eve, right?"

"Yes."

"Then you can panic that morning for ten minutes. Set a timer if you need to. Ten minutes, then pull up your socks and get to work aweing that room full of people who have the power to make your dreams come true."

"But that's the rub, Soph." Hailey stopped the swinging bench and turned in her seat to face her sister head-on. "I've been playing New York clubs for almost four years. If my voice is as amazing and unique as Ryan thinks it is, why haven't I caught anyone's eye before now? My video went viral, but no one has been trying to bang down the door to get to me. I'm not convinced that anything will come of this. I'm worried that I'll start to believe in myself the way Ryan does and end up massively disappointed when it leads nowhere."

"He invited his friend from Remmy specifically to hear you sing, right?"

"Yeah."

"Then you have reason to hope. You're not just hoping to be

noticed this time. There will be someone there with the sole intention of figuring out if you're worth taking a chance on or not. And for the record, I think he's going to be blown away." Sophie leaned over, pulling Hailey into a hug. "Now can we go eat? Mom announced dinner like twenty minutes ago, and I'm famished."

"You were snacking on a roll when you came out here."

"Blame the baby. I'm hungry *always*."

Hailey laughed, getting off the swing before turning to help her sister up. "Thanks for listening."

"You know I'm here for you. But can I give you one last piece of advice?"

"Sure."

"Next time Kendra's hot uncle wants to chat with you, don't act like you aren't interested. You don't know what's going to happen, or where you'll be a month from now. So don't decide that you're meant to fail before you even give it a chance."

"That's a good speech. Maybe next time Ryan wants to hang out with me I'll call you and make you repeat it."

Sophie grabbed her arm. "He wanted to hang out? What did you do?"

"Nothing. I went home."

Sophie rolled her eyes. "You're hopeless."

That's *exactly* what she was afraid of.

CHAPTER SIXTEEN

Hailey gripped her guitar case, moving it to the other hand as her sweaty palm made the handle slick. It was going to be fine. She was going to do fine. If she told herself that enough times it was bound to be true, right?

She had taken Nikki over to the Martinezes' house earlier to settle her in with Kendra and had left as Nikki was pulling out sparkly Play-doh and asking Kendra which bug they should form first. They were clearly going to have a good time.

But Hailey didn't know if the same would be true for her. She tried to tell herself that she didn't need to worry. She was background music, meant to be tucked into the corner of the little boutique-y event floor, playing low music as rich music executives and magazine bigwigs drank and socialized. She had gone to the Granger Studio the night before for a soundcheck and practiced a slow song and an upbeat, traditional one, and they'd both sounded great.

Tonight would not be any different.

Tugging at the bottom of her sparkly silver dress, Hailey waited for the elevator doors to open on the right floor of the Granger Studio and stepped onto the waxed hardwood floor.

Tables were set up for dinner around the room, leaving space for people to talk and gather between them. Long, wide-open windows lined the walls overlooking lower Manhattan and the Hudson River, the water beginning to glow orange from the setting sun.

People in black pants and white button-down shirts milled around the room, lighting chafing dishes and setting tables.

Hailey weaved through the tables to the back of the room where a small dais was set up with a stool and a mic, and she set down her guitar.

"Hailey?"

Chills ran down her neck. Straightening, she turned to find Ryan standing behind her, one hand in his pocket, the other holding his phone. She hadn't seen him since the week before when she went to his apartment to set up his tree, and *wow*, she'd forgotten how handsome he was. Or maybe that was just the sleek black tux cut perfectly to his waist and defining all of his best features.

"Hey," she croaked, unable to spit out intelligible words. Had someone melted him and poured him into that suit? Because there was no other way it could fit him so well.

"You look amazing," he said, slipping his phone into his pocket and crossing the floor to pause in front of her. His eyebrows rose and his eyes fell, his gaze sweeping over her gown in a swift motion. "Are you feeling ready?"

Hailey started to nod but shifted to shaking her head. "I don't know. My songs are ready, but I'm so nervous."

"You have nothing to worry about. This isn't your first performance, and you're going to do great. If you get anxious just look for me in the crowd. I'll pull a funny face or something."

She smiled at the image that provoked. "So you want to make me laugh in the middle of my songs?"

"Well, I wanted to make you smile now, and it worked, didn't it?"

Hailey's smile deepened.

Ryan matched her grin. "People should start arriving in the next five minutes or so. Do you want to start now so you're playing when they get here?"

"Sure thing, boss."

He wrinkled his nose. "Nope. Don't like that."

"What? Boss?"

"Yeah. It sounds weird coming from you."

Hailey laughed. "Okay."

She turned to pull out her guitar and put away the case, and Ryan slipped away. It was smart to start playing now. She needed to warm up her voice anyway. Hailey sat on the stool, resting one wedged heel against the lowest rung to give her guitar somewhere to sit, and did a quick tune to make sure everything was in order. Her heart raced, but so far nothing had gone wrong.

She hoped the rest of the evening would go as smoothly.

Guests began arriving halfway into her third song, and it was all Hailey could do to keep singing and not analyze Ryan's reaction to the guests. It occurred to her that she had no idea who this Joe from Remmy Records even was or what he looked like. She'd been so focused on preparing her songs, that she was now wholly unprepared for who the scout was going to be.

Shoving that thought to the back of her head, she continued singing, playing her guitar, and watching the influx of guests arrive at the New Year's Eve Fiftieth Anniversary party of *Sound Magazine*. Wow, Ryan must be incredibly proud of everything he and his father had accomplished in the last fifty years.

The room grew warmer as the crowd swelled, and Hailey did her best to lose herself in the music, to keep her focus on strumming strings and familiar chords. She slipped from one song into the next, pausing only when she needed to sip her water.

Her gaze was trained on the floor in front of her, focusing on the chord changes when shiny, black shoes stepped into her line of sight, pointed right at her. She lifted her gaze to find Ryan beaming at her, and her entire body reciprocated in kind without missing a beat of the song. He looked so proud, so thrilled, that she couldn't help but feel like maybe she had been doing exactly as good as he'd expected her to.

When the song came to a close, she lowered her heel to the floor to give her leg a break, holding onto her guitar to keep it from slipping to the floor.

"Hey, Hailey, I've got someone I'd like you to meet."

The crowd continued to chat and socialize as though they hadn't noticed the music coming to an end, and Hailey smiled at Ryan. Was this it? Was he about to introduce her to the man who would make her music dreams come true?

"Hailey, this is Joanna Swenson from Remmy Records." He pulled a blonde woman forward, resting his arm on her back.

Hailey froze. Steel-blue eyes stared at her, framed by a perfect blonde bob. *This* was Joe from Remmy Records? The short, gorgeous woman who'd stopped by Ryan's apartment and had been flustered and annoyed to find another woman there? Probably *Jo*, she corrected mentally. Joanna. She kicked herself for not inviting Jo in and forcing the woman to understand that things between Ryan and herself were nonexistent.

But that wouldn't be entirely true. Hailey did have feelings for Ryan. She just knew nothing would ever come of them.

"We've met," Joanna said, unamused.

Ryan's eyebrows pulled together. "You have?"

"Yes. At your apartment the other night." She shot Ryan an accusatory glare before turning back and sticking a hand out to shake Hailey's. Hailey shook her hand, trying to keep her expression neutral. "You have a very unique voice."

"Thank you." Hailey was shocked the woman didn't storm away.

"Ryan says you're interested in pursuing a career with Remmy?"

She swallowed. "It would be a dream come true."

Jo nodded, narrowing her eyes. "I'll be listening closely this evening. Show me everything you've got."

So she was still giving Hailey a chance? Hailey nodded, trying to smile, but her emotions were as tight as the skyline shimmering through the darkened windows. "You got it."

Taking Ryan's hand, Jo turned and pulled him away. He watched Hailey over his shoulder, confusion marring his brow, but she swiftly looked down at her guitar, trying to decide the best thing to play to impress Jo.

She started strumming the intro for a song she'd written earlier that year and forced herself to watch the windows in the back of the room. Lights twinkled from nearby buildings and the river ahead of them, and if she blurred her eyes just right, she could remove the image from her head of Jo pulling Ryan away by the hand. It was such a familiar gesture that it stuck in her throat like a glob of peanut butter.

Hailey shook her head and started singing. She had only known Ryan for a few short weeks. It didn't matter that it had seemed like longer, or that she imagined they were like souls with a greater understanding of one another. She was just attracted to the guy. That was all. It wasn't something deeper like she'd led herself to believe.

And she'd prove that by forgetting all about him and singing her heart out.

"I thought you said this was a brand-new artist and you'd never heard of her before like a week ago?" Jo's eyes sparked, and she had a bite to her words.

Ryan didn't know why Jo was angry, but he knew he needed to put out the fire before Hailey's chances were ruined. "It's true."

She shifted on her hip, staring out over the Hudson. "Then why was she at your apartment last week?"

"At my..." Ah. So Jo was the stranger who'd stopped by when Hailey was setting up Christmas in his home. "She works for Amber, my sister. She's her nanny. I asked her to walk Sergeant for me since I was stuck at the office. It was nothing."

But that wasn't true, was it? What he felt for Hailey wasn't *nothing*. But he couldn't exactly say that to Jo now. Not when he recognized the bitter jealousy in her gaze. They'd been broken up for a year. He'd hoped she was over him.

"Does my personal life have anything to do with whether or not you'll sign her?"

"That depends," Jo said, stepping closer and taking his tie in her hand. She dropped her voice to a low, velvety tone. "How do you feel about her?"

Hailey's voice rang over the speakers, so clear and beautiful, exactly like her heart. She was incredible, and she deserved this chance, regardless of how he felt about her.

Ryan stepped out of Jo's hold. "The Jo I know is more professional than that."

She looked stung. Closing her eyes, she shook her head and drew in a breath. "You're right. I don't know why I'm feeling so possessive. Maybe it's just regret that we didn't work out. You know how the holidays have always stressed me out."

He took her hand. "I do. I'll always care about you, Jo, but not in that way."

She gave him a wry smile. "The girl has talent, I'll give you that. But I don't know what I'm going to do yet."

"Just give her a fair shot. She hasn't done anything wrong here, and I think she could be really great."

Jo glanced over her shoulder to watch Hailey, and Ryan let himself do the same. She was a natural. Jo would be an idiot to let talent like hers walk away.

Sighing, she turned back to him. "We'll see, I guess." She spun on her heel and walked away.

Ryan leaned against the brick wall, sliding his hands into his pockets and watching Hailey perform as Carter sidled up beside him.

"She's good," Carter said.

"I know."

"She single?" he asked.

Ryan whipped his head around but stopped himself from reacting when he noticed the amusement dancing in his friend's eyes. "Am I that obvious?"

"Yeah. You can't stop staring at her like she's the most incredible thing to walk the earth."

"What if she is?"

Carter shrugged. "Then don't let her go, I guess?"

He shrugged. "I can't move back to LA."

Carter put up both his hands. "Yeah man, you're in a tough spot. I've got no advice for you there."

The next song came to a close and Sarah took the stage, thanking Hailey for playing and dismissing her—as they'd previously agreed—for her break. Ryan slipped around the edge of the crowd as people began taking their seats and snuck into the kitchen and through to the back hallway, finding Hailey leaning against the wall, her head resting against the brick and her eyes closed.

He crossed toward her, coming to stop right in front of her. "You are amazing."

Her eyes shot open, widening as they rested on him. "Jo is a *woman*?"

Ryan faltered, stepping back a little. "Yes. Did I not tell you that?"

"No. You just called her Jo, so I made the crazy leap that she was a man."

"It's not that crazy of a leap..." He caught her withering stare and stopped. "I'm sorry. I didn't realize it would bother you."

Hailey closed her eyes. "It didn't bother me. I just..." She looked right at him, screwing up her nose in apology. "I don't know. She stopped by your apartment when I was setting up the tree, and it was awkward. She clearly didn't like seeing another woman there, and I didn't try hard enough to explain that there's nothing going on between us."

"Maybe that's a good thing." He stepped closer, his fingers skimming her arm and taking hold of her free hand, her other one securely fastened to the neck of her guitar. "Maybe it would have been a lie."

Hailey's eyes widened, her hand tightening in his. Her lips parted and he glanced at them, unable to tear his gaze away. He started to lean forward, his body closing in on hers as his lips moved on their own accord.

"You just got out of a bad relationship," she whispered, halting him in his tracks.

"What? No, I didn't." He was so close now he could feel her breath on his lips.

"Amber told me you left a toxic relationship behind in LA... that you were only looking for a rebound."

He looked in her eyes, holding them in his so she would understand the truth of his words. "I broke up with Jo a year ago, and it's been long over. There's no rebound here. This is all real."

Hailey sucked in a breath. "Really?" she whispered. "*Jo* was the girlfriend?"

He chuckled softly, the sound more of a rumble. "I promise you, it does not make a difference. She's really professional."

"She's still a woman."

"Hailey? You're on," a voice called from down the hall, causing them both to freeze.

Hailey pulled her hand from his and turned her head, clearing her throat softly. "Thanks."

Ryan leaned forward, resting his forehead against the wall and feeling her heartbeat erratically in her chest, pressed against his. His body hummed with the energy pulsing between them, but the mood was dead from the interruption, and he pushed away from the wall, giving Hailey space to go.

She started down the hall, and he watched her retreat. "Meet me here when you're off?"

She looked over her shoulder. "Deal."

CHAPTER SEVENTEEN

Hailey nestled her guitar into its case and gripped the handle, sweeping her gaze over the empty room littered with remnants of the event. She'd done well, she thought, but now she was wiped out and looking forward to getting out of her tight dress and falling into her bed.

Jo hadn't said anything to her before leaving, and Hailey wasn't sure if that was something to worry about or not, so she tried to shove it from her mind. She'd watched Jo talk to Amber and Luis before she left the event well before midnight, and they'd all glanced at Hailey, but she'd been singing and couldn't exactly jump off the stage and run over to them, demanding to know what they were saying about her.

Cool it, Hailey. She drew in a deep breath and walked through the bustling kitchen, letting herself into the back hallway. Her heart hammered in her chest when her gaze fell on Ryan waiting at the end of the hall, leaning against the wall with his hands in his pockets like he had patiently waited for her all night.

Hailey's pulse thrummed harder the closer she got to him. "What's up?" *Wow. Could you sound any less chill?*

"Can I give you a ride home?" he asked. "I drove tonight."

KASEY STOCKTON

"Sure."

He reached for her guitar case and opened the door at the end of the hall, letting a gust of winter wind steal into the space and send chills over her skin. She zipped up her coat, stepping past Ryan and down the long set of stairs that led to a back alley lined with cars.

Ryan unlocked the trunk of a black sedan and slid her guitar into the back before facing her. "Want to go for a walk?"

"In this weather?"

"It'll be quick." He seemed eager, and she didn't have the heart to turn him down. Besides, she really couldn't complain about spending more time with him. Maybe he'd talked to Jo and knew something. He took her hand and led her down the street and around the corner to a set of stairs, indicating that she precede him.

"Where are we going?"

"Have you never walked the High Line?" he asked, climbing the rickety metal stairs behind her.

She looked down at him over her shoulder. "I've never heard of it."

"And you call yourself a New Yorker."

She laughed. "Actually I don't. I've only lived here four years."

"Long enough to spend some time in the West Village, I think."

Hailey shook her head, laughing as she reached the top of the stairs. It was a walking path raised high above the street. There were a few stragglers down the walkway, but it was mostly deserted. "What is this place?"

Ryan pointed to a set of railway tracks half-covered by the paved walkway. "It used to be an above-ground railway to get people around the city. But now it's just a cool walkway up in the air."

"It's beautiful." Hailey gazed over the water shining in the distance, New York Harbor reflecting the lights of the buildings butting against it, and then to the lights of the buildings across the water. Ryan's hand slid over hers and he tugged her along.

"It can get crowded during the day with tourists, but when it's cold they tend to stay away."

"Exactly how I like it," Hailey said.

She shivered, and Ryan paused, turning toward her. "It's freezing. Maybe this wasn't a good idea."

"It's fine. Walking will warm me."

He nodded. "You did great tonight."

"Thanks. Let's hope Jo thinks so, too."

"She didn't say anything to you before she left?"

"No. Was she supposed to?"

He sounded confused. "I don't know. Maybe she needs time to think. Did anyone approach you?"

"Surprisingly enough, no one rushed the stage demanding the chance to represent me."

"That's so weird." Ryan chuckled. "Jo told me she liked you."

"Please don't get my hopes up."

"Fine, I'll say no more." He sent her a crooked smile. "But that won't stop me from nudging her later."

Hailey bumped his shoulder with hers. "I won't say no to a little nudging. As long as it doesn't send her the other way."

Ryan's voice was dry. "I have a feeling that offering you a chance to move across the country is appealing to her right now."

"Yeah." But how did Hailey feel about that? Was she willing to give up her life here, this guy, and Kendra to chase a dream?

Yes. The answer was yes.

"Would you go?" he asked, meeting her eyes, pulling on her arm so she paused, too. "If Jo offers you a contract, will you move to LA?"

Hailey held his gaze. "Yes."

He nodded, his eyes growing serious. "I thought as much."

She lifted a shoulder. "It's my dream. If I get a chance, I'm taking it. Even if it would be hard to leave."

"Hard to leave Kenny?"

"Among other things," she said, her breath clouding before her.

Ryan's knuckles brushed against her cheekbone, his thumb moving to trace her jaw until his fingers rested around her neck. Chills ran down her shoulders, her skin heating from his touch. "And here I thought I'd just met the woman of my dreams, and she's about to leave me."

"We don't know that yet," Hailey whispered. For all they knew, Jo wouldn't offer her anything, and she'd remain Kendra's nanny forever.

"So do we pretend, just for tonight, that you aren't going anywhere?" he asked.

"Yes." Her hands slid up his coat, gripping his collar as his other arm went around her waist, pulling her tightly against him.

Ryan's forehead came down to rest against hers, their breath mingling. "It's not just your voice, you know. I think *you* are incredible."

Hailey sucked in a breath of surprise, his words reaching her heart and wrapping it in an embrace. Tugging on his coat, she pulled him closer, touching her lips to his.

Ryan reacted immediately, pressing her closer to him as he deepened the kiss, pouring heat into her body with the touch of his lips. He buried his fingers in her hair, tilting her head this way, then that, until she melted, and her legs refused to hold her up.

Hailey backed up, sucking in a breath of air before sliding her hands over his chest and pulling his neck to bring him closer again. She could not seem to get enough of Ryan, and she didn't want it to end.

A whistle sounded like a catcall and they broke apart, grinning at each other as a group of teenagers passed them.

"Getting high on the high line?" one of the kids asked.

Ryan held her gaze. "Ignore them."

"It's not untrue." She laughed. "But not high the way they think." She felt like she was floating on happiness, instead.

But maybe that wasn't a good idea. Not until they knew what the future held. "I think I need to get home."

"Probably a good idea," Ryan agreed. "I would keep you up here all night if it was up to me."

Hailey didn't know if that made things better or worse, but she took Ryan's hand and started back toward the steps that would lead them to his car.

CHAPTER EIGHTEEN

The meeting was today, and Ryan shook with nervous energy.
He'd texted Hailey off and on over the last few days, and she
still hadn't heard anything from Jo. He needed to reach out to
his ex-girlfriend, but he didn't have the time. Once the meeting
was over, though, he would.

He just needed to win back Bradshaw's account first.

Amber stepped into his office, glancing around. "It hasn't
changed much since Dad worked in here."

"Yeah, I haven't had time for a makeover yet."

She shrugged. "Keep it. Dad had good taste."

"Do you feel ready?" Ryan asked.

Amber pulled out her phone and absently scrolled. "It's
Bradshaw. He's known us since we were in diapers. I don't
know why you're so worried."

"Because this is business. Relationships can only get you so
far. He's not going to throw his money away on something that
won't give him a return."

Amber rolled her eyes, following him from the office and
down to the board room. They set up for the meeting and were
waiting when Bradshaw finally arrived in a slick suit, his hair

combed over a shiny scalp. He shook Ryan's hand and accepted a hug from Amber before they each took their seats.

"How's your mother?" Bradshaw asked.

"She's happy down in Orlando," Amber said. "She just flew home yesterday, actually. We got to have her here for the holidays."

"I'm sorry to have missed her. I always enjoy seeing your mother." His ruddy cheeks rounded in a smile. "It takes me back quite a ways, you know."

"Of course."

Bradshaw leaned back in his chair, narrowing his gaze on Ryan. "So you want me to let you keep my ad account for your failing magazine. Show me why I should take a chance on you."

Amber seemed to freeze beside Ryan, and he knew a moment of pride that he'd guessed exactly how this meeting was going to go. He pulled out his PowerPoint clicker and began his presentation.

It took all of thirty minutes to show the increase in their numbers since he'd taken the helm at *Sound Magazine* and his ideas and projections on how it would continue to grow. He had a good team, they had only been missing a decent leader. And somehow, Ryan fit the role.

He'd made the executive decision not to critique videos on YouTube anymore—something about Hailey's hurt had made him second-guess that avenue—but he had other ideas for the channel to promote traffic to the online portion of the magazine. Not to mention that the special New Year's Eve edition had only been live for two days and had already surpassed sales and clicks from every other edition in the last three years.

Bradshaw, however, didn't reveal a stitch of feeling throughout the entire presentation.

Amber delivered her spiel for her portion of the ad account— her fashion magazine—and Carter, who came in late, explained how he planned to shift the vibe of the magazine to fit a younger audience in order to stay relevant.

They completed the presentation to silence, Bradshaw chewing his cheek as he gazed past Ryan's head. It took every fiber of control Ryan had not to pound his fist on the table and demand an answer right away. His heart hummed and his fingers tapped his leg restlessly underneath the table.

"You know," Bradshaw said, drawing out the words excruciatingly slowly. "I almost felt for a minute like I was thrown back thirty years, and it was your father up there convincing me to take a chance on him. You've got his flair, Ryan. It sounds like you inherited his brain, too."

Bradshaw stood, and Ryan followed suit, chair legs scraping the floor as everyone rose. "We'll renew with you. I like where things are heading."

All of Ryan's breath left his lungs in one fell swoop, and his entire body relaxed. He reached forward to shake Bradshaw's hand, hoping he wouldn't crumple into a pile on the floor.

"I'll have my office get in touch, and we'll sign by the end of the week."

"Great." Ryan did his best to sound professional. "Thank you."

"Hey, don't thank me." Bradshaw smiled. "I haven't handed you anything. You earned this."

Ryan watched the man walk out of his office. He pulled out his phone while Amber began gathering her things. The first thing he wanted to do was send Hailey a text to let her know he'd gotten the account, but he needed to do something else first.

Stepping into the hall, he dialed Jo's number and put the phone to his ear.

"Hey." She answered right away. "I'm about to get on a plane. Is it urgent?"

"I just wanted to touch base with you about Hailey Grant. I haven't heard anything."

"Hailey? She's not interested in a contract. I did try, though, so don't throw rocks at me or anything."

Not interested? That morning her mournful report had been that she still hadn't heard anything from Jo—followed shortly by forcing Ryan to promise not to interfere. He broke the promise now, but what good were contacts if he wasn't going to use them?

"She told you that?" Ryan asked.

Muffled announcements through an intercom sounded through the speaker. "I have to go, Ryan."

"Just answer me, please. Hailey turned you down?"

"She never reached out to me. I told Amber to have her call me, and I've heard nothing. She had seventy-two hours, which I thought was really generous of me."

Ryan closed his eyes, pinching the bridge of his nose. Amber was going to answer for this. "If she never got the message, what then? Does she still have a chance to accept your offer?"

Jo was silent, but the sound of people and speakers in the background proved she hadn't hung up yet.

"Jo, please?"

"Fine, Ryan. She has until I land in LA. If I have a message on my phone, I'll consider it."

Relief relaxed his shoulders. "Thanks, Jo."

She laughed. "You always were a weakness of mine."

Ryan smiled. "Safe travels."

"Thanks." She hung up the phone, and Ryan turned back toward the boardroom.

"Hey, Amber." He slipped his phone back into his pocket, tamping down frustration. "Want to explain why Jo thinks Hailey isn't interested in a contract with Remmy Records?"

Amber froze, glancing from Carter to Ryan.

Carter lifted his hands, walking from the room. "I'm out."

Her eyes wide, she tilted her head to the side. "Come on. You know I don't want to lose my nanny."

His stomach wound tight, disbelief forcing a scoff from his throat. "So you jeopardized her career?"

"If she really loved Kendra, she wouldn't—"

"Are you serious, Amber?" It took all of Ryan's self-control not to leap over the table and yell at his sister. "You think Hailey doesn't love Kendra if she decides to chase her dream? That's beyond selfish of you."

Her eyes were hard but laced with panic. Did she even realize how horrible her actions were? "You don't understand, Ryan. You don't have kids."

"Maybe not, but I do know I wouldn't try to get in the way of someone else's success like that. It's just low, Amber."

She closed her eyes, rubbing over her eyebrows with her fingertips. "I know. But when Jo told us her plans and asked me to pass it on to Hailey, I freaked out. I really don't want to lose her."

"It looks like you might anyway."

She glanced up sharply. "Are you going to tell her what I did?"

"No. I think you should."

Amber held his gaze. "You're actually into her, aren't you?"

"I am."

She threw her arms out to the sides. "Then why aren't you trying harder to keep her in New York?"

"Because I care about her more than that."

Amber rolled her eyes. "Fine. Go. Tell her everything. I don't think I can."

"I really think this should come from you."

She sank down into her seat, frowning. "Well, it won't. So I guess it's up to you."

He nodded and turned to leave the room. This was something he wanted to do in person.

The Central Park Zoo and its leaf cutter ants had been everything Kendra had dreamed they would be, and now she lay asleep, cuddled by Hailey on the sofa as *A Bug's Life* played on the TV in front of them. The elevator dinged to let them know someone was coming, and Hailey craned her neck to see who it was.

She'd been trying to tell herself over the last few days that it was fine that Jo didn't offer her a contract and that she wasn't totally crushed. Both of which were horrible, huge lies.

But Ryan and his sweet texts had been a balm over the sting of rejection, of course.

When he stepped through the kitchen and caught her gaze, her entire body felt lighter. She smiled at him, and he motioned to her, whispering. "Can you sneak away for a second?"

She took a pillow from the end of the sofa and carefully lifted Kendra's head, sliding the pillow underneath her as Hailey scooted down the cushion. She got up, tiptoeing from the room and into the kitchen, the movie playing softly in the background. Ryan leaned against the counter, so she rested her hands on the island, leaving the large slab of granite between them.

"Did you get the account?" she asked.

He grinned. "Yes."

Hailey squealed before slapping her hand over her mouth, her eyes going wide. She waited a second but didn't hear any stirring, so she must not have woken Kendra. Lowering her voice, she whispered. "Congrats! I can't imagine how relieved you must be."

"Immensely, of course. But that's not all."

"What happened?"

"I talked to Jo."

Hailey stiffened. Ryan's face was a work of stone, and she couldn't tell if he was about to deliver good news or bad.

His voice was steady. "There was a mix-up, and—"

"A mix-up?"

He cleared his throat. "Yes. It turns out that Jo asked my sister to have you call her if you were interested in pursuing a contract with Remmy."

Hailey's breath caught, and the marble floor felt like it fell away. "But Amber never said anything to me."

Ryan's gaze flicked to the living room behind her. "Because of Kendra."

"But..." Her brain wouldn't wrap around the situation. She closed her eyes, running it through her head. "So Amber *intentionally* didn't tell me."

"She didn't want to lose you. If it matters, I do think she's ashamed of what she did."

Hailey scoffed, anger and confusion warring within her. Her hands gripped the counter tightly, her knuckles turning white. "So what now? Have I missed my shot?"

"Jo said you have until she lands in LA to leave her a message with your interest and she'll consider it within the window of her initial offer."

The breath left her lungs in one fell swoop, and she turned around, leaning against the island, and dropped her head in her hands. This was it. Her dreams were about to be realized. She could uproot her entire life, move across the country, and chase a music career.

Strong arms came around her as Ryan pulled her against him, and she slid her arms around his waist, resting her forehead against his collar bone.

Could she do it? Could she leave her family, Kendra, Nikki, and this amazing guy?

It would be so, *so* hard. But she thought she could. No, she knew she could.

"What are you going to do?" he asked.

She leaned back, looking him in the eye. "I'm going to do it. I'm going to tell her yes."

His eyes were sad, but he smiled. "Good."

"I don't think it's the end of the world. We can stay in touch. I know I'll need your advice every step of the way. If you're willing to stay my friend, that is." And she would not have to live in LA *forever*.

"Your friend?" He shook his head. "I don't think I'm willing to do that."

Her heart sank, and her arms slackened their hold, but Ryan tightened his. He bent his head to see directly into her eyes. "If you'll have me, I want to be *much* more than just your friend."

"I'm moving across the country."

"Not for forever. We can fly to see each other, and once things get under control with *Sound* I'll be able to do ninety percent of my job remotely."

Hailey's body stilled. She was unable to believe what she was hearing. "You want to try a long-distance relationship?"

"I want to *try*. Whatever that looks like. I'm not willing to give you up quite yet. I just got you."

Hailey stood up on tiptoes and pressed her lips to Ryan's, her heart thudding as he returned the kiss.

When he pulled away, his grin was wide. "So that's a yes?"

She nodded. "Can I get Jo's number from you?"

"Absolutely." He pulled out his phone and sent the contact to her, watching her as she dialed the number and stepped into the foyer to leave her message.

She had no idea what the future held at this point, but she was pretty glad she'd have the chance to find out.

CHAPTER NINETEEN

Hailey sat on the floor of Kendra's room, fishing through the canvas bag holding the Bug Bingo pieces before pulling one out. "Caddis Fly."

Kendra squealed. "Yes! I have that one." She chose a green tile from the pile on the floor and placed it on her bingo card, grinning up at Hailey. "One more square and I'll have Bingo. I think I'm going to win."

"I could still win. Stranger things have happened."

Kendra took the bag and dug into it, pulling out another tile. "Vampire moth."

"I don't have it."

"Me, neither." Kendra found the vampire moth on the master-key board and put the tile down before handing the bag to Hailey.

It had been a week since Hailey had left a message on Jo's phone, and they had spent time going back and forth about contract details and negotiating. Ryan really knew his stuff, and his lawyer was even better. She didn't know she would have managed to secure a good deal for herself without her team.

She took the canvas bag of pieces and reached forward to brush Kendra's hair out of her face. The hardest part about taking this contract was leaving Kendra. "Hey, how about we put this game away after the first person gets a Bingo and go downstairs for some hot chocolate?"

"Okay. Now draw a piece."

Hailey chuckled. "Stag beetle."

"Yes! Bingo!" Hailey put a green marker on her bingo card before she jumped to her feet and did a happy dance.

"Well done, Ken. Now help me get the game put away."

"Should we play until blackout?"

Hailey lifted an eyebrow. "Hot chocolate or blackout? I don't think we have time for both."

"Okay, hot chocolate." Kendra grinned, dropping to her knees to gather the green marker pieces and put them back in the Bug Bingo box. Her phone buzzed and she pulled it from her pocket, reading the text.

Ryan: *Dinner tonight? I can meet you at Amber's, and we can go from there.*

Hailey: *Sounds great. Can't wait to see you.*

Ryan: *I'm grinning right now.*

Hailey: *Pics or it didn't happen.*

Kendra crawled over, putting her face between Hailey and the phone. "Who are you texting?"

Hailey slapped her phone against her chest, her cheeks warming. "Your uncle Ryan." She reached for the bingo boards and stacked them in the box, shutting the lid and carrying the game to Kendra's closet.

"Do you love him?" Kendra asked, her tiny voice thoughtful.

Hailey put the game on the shelf and fixed a smile on her face. She didn't know if she loved Ryan or not, but she imagined that one day she would. She followed Kendra from the room, and they made their way downstairs to the kitchen. "I care about him."

Amber stood near the fridge, her arms crossed over her chest and her eyes fixed on Hailey. "Ken, run and get your pajamas on."

"But Mom, it's not bedtime yet."

Amber's brows lifted. "Now, please."

"I'll get your hot chocolate ready while you're upstairs," Hailey said. Kendra nodded before leaving the kitchen and the awkward, thick silence hanging around the women. They'd seen one another in passing all week but never had Amber tried to talk like this, and Hailey felt the discomfort of it in her bones. She was still upset by Amber's actions. The woman hadn't even apologized for trying to hold Hailey back. Not really.

"Ryan tells me that you have your plane ticket now."

Hailey nodded. "I leave in ten days. I emailed you about—"

"I know." She swatted her hand, shaking her head. "I've begun interviewing replacements already. My mom might come up and help me in the interim."

"I wish I could stay longer."

"It's fine. We'd have to replace you either way." She sighed, drawing the sound out. What was the point of this awkward conversation? Guilt-tripping?

Hailey crossed to the cupboards and pulled out two mugs. Looking over her shoulder, she caught Amber's eye on her. "Should I make you some hot chocolate too?"

Amber shook her head. "Listen, we need to talk. I really...I just..." Scrubbing a hand over her eyes, she looked up with resolve. "I want to apologize for what I did. I'm just embarrassed that I stooped so low. You have a right to be angry with me, but I hope one day you can come to forgive me. I don't want Kendra to lose you forever over my stupidity."

Setting the cups down, Hailey turned around and leaned against the counter. That could not have been easy for Amber to admit her faults, or to apologize, and Hailey immediately felt a lightening of her spirit, as though the gross negative feelings that had been weighing her down were now gone.

"I forgive you."

Amber's face relaxed. "Oh, good. I really...I just think about what I did, and it makes me sick to my stomach. I can't believe I played with your life like that."

"Kenny's special. I understand wanting to protect her from anything in her life changing." Maybe not to the extent of trying to sabotage someone's career, but that was officially in the past now.

"Not that I expect this to make up for it at all, but Luis and I got you a little going-away present." She stepped forward, digging through her purse, and pulled out a long, white envelope. "I don't know if you want to use it for a new wardrobe when you get to LA to impress all those music execs, or if you want to use it to get an apartment, or whatever. It's yours."

Hailey took the envelope, her chest robbed of air, and slipped it open. The number of zeros on the end of the check knocked her back. She sought Amber's eyes. "You don't have to do this."

"We want to. Think of it as a bonus for taking such good care of Kenny and a show of goodwill. I really do wish you the best, Hailey."

Hailey's eyes welled up with warm tears and she dashed them away, crossing the kitchen to pull Amber into a hug. "Thank you. And thank Luis for me, too. This is too kind of you both."

Amber returned the hug then leaned back, awkwardly smiling. "Sure thing. Now that I'm home, do you want to take off early tonight?"

"How about we all share hot chocolate first?"

A warm smile curved her lips, her eyes suspiciously shiny. "That sounds great to me."

By the time Hailey, Kendra, and Amber had finished their hot chocolate, it was nearing evening. Hailey hugged them both goodbye and slipped on her coat, warm satisfaction resting on her heart. Amber was only human, and her effort to make an apology was a balm to Hailey's nerves. Leaving the east coast, moving to a city she had never even been to before, was a huge step for her. Having an emergency stash of money to fall back on, or to give her wardrobe a facelift, was a comfort.

Punching in her code to bring up the elevator, Hailey sighed, lowering her shoulders. She hadn't realized what a weight they had carried before, but reconciliation had a way of lightening her soul, restoring balance to her equilibrium.

Beeping sounded through the foyer and the doors slid open, revealing a handsome, dark-haired man leaning back against the wall, his eyes on his phone. Ryan. He glanced up, straightening, and paused when his eyes met hers.

She put a hand out to hold the elevator doors open. "Do you want to come in?"

Shaking his head, he took her hand and pulled her into the elevator, his skin warming hers. "That's okay. I'm coming back tomorrow to have dinner with them."

Ryan's hands slid around her waist and she had to pull her purse higher on her shoulder to avoid him knocking it to the ground. The doors slid closed behind her, and Ryan reached over to hit the button to take them down.

In his arms, she was whole, her heart racing in rhythm with his, and her mind at peace.

"I've been wanting to do this for a while," Ryan said, pulling her close and pressing his lips to hers.

She smiled beneath his kiss, her hands tightening on his coat. Pulling away, she laughed. "You do that all the time."

"But not under mistletoe." He quirked a brow, and Hailey glanced up, finding the dried mistletoe hanging on the elevator ceiling, the red ribbon wound around it.

"How is that still there?"

"I don't know. Someone must have forgotten they put it up." His smile grew mischievous. "So let's not let it go to waste."

"I'm pretty sure it's been dead for a while. Do we still kiss if the mistletoe is dead?"

Ryan laughed, and the doors opened. He pulled her close and kissed her hard. "You're one of a kind, Hailey Grant."

EPILOGUE

TWO YEARS LATER

Hailey stepped off the plane at JFK and traveled down to baggage claim as fast as her stiff legs would carry her. She wasn't quite at the point where everyone recognized her yet, but she still got stopped occasionally for an autograph, and right now she was in too much of a hurry to stop for anything.

She stepped through the doors and made a straight line for the right carousel. She scanned the crowds for the tall, dark, super-hot guy who was supposed to be waiting for her.

When her eyes caught Ryan's, she broke into a run, jumping into his arms and wrapping her legs around his waist. He leaned up to kiss her and she squeezed his neck, kissing him back.

"Ew, Hailey! Gross."

The young voice broke through her euphoric thoughts, and she leaned back, grinning at the man she loved with all her heart. "You brought Kendra?"

Ryan laughed. "You think she would let me leave her home?"

Hailey disentangled herself from Ryan's grip, lowering her feet to the floor and turning toward the little eight-year-old she loved dearly.

Kendra wrinkled her nose. "You aren't going to kiss me too, right?"

"You bet I am." Hailey pulled Kendra in for a hug, loving the squeeze of the girl's small arms around her waist, and dropped a kiss on the top of her head.

"Did you check a bag?" Ryan asked.

"Yes. Light blue with a bright green ribbon."

He went to watch for her suitcase, and Hailey turned back to Kendra. "So, how are things going with Rachael?"

"Will you be sad if I tell you that I love my new nanny?"

"Not at all, you goose. That's what I want for you. Heaven knows you've tried enough of them."

Kendra rolled her eyes. "Most of them are fine, but Mom is picky."

Hailey lifted her eyebrows. "And this one passes all the tests?"

"So far," Kendra said, her smile hopeful. "I think she's here to stay."

Ryan came up behind them with the correct suitcase and took Hailey's hand. "We ready to go home?"

"Yes."

He leaned over and kissed her again. Taking her hand, he brought it up and kissed the finger holding her wedding ring. "Good. Because we've missed you here. That tour was eternally long."

She squeezed his hand. "I saw you three weeks ago."

Ryan grinned. "That three weeks was torture. Next time sign me up as a roadie because I'm coming along on the whole thing."

"You could, you know. You can always work out of the bus."

He held her gaze. "Maybe I will."

"Can we go see the leaf cutter ants this week?" Kendra asked.

"Yes. But I was thinking we could go see the Natural History

Museum, too. And I found an insect exhibit down in SoHo that's only going to be here for a few weeks, so we need to hit that first."

Kendra looked up at Hailey. "Can we bring Rachael?"

"The nanny?" Ryan asked.

"Absolutely." Hailey smiled. "The more, the merrier."

Ryan squeezed her fingers, and she smiled up at him like a lovesick fool.

She never thought she would end up being so grateful for a critique.

Snowflake Wishes

She needs to save her diner. He has orders to kick her out.

Madison Bell has tried everything to keep her diner from failing in the small town of Holly Springs. When a handsome stranger shows up just before Christmas should she trust his marketing advice or keep doing things her own way?

Jake Tyler has two motivations for traveling to the tiny town of Holly Springs: he needs to learn why his parents have kept him from his grandmother his whole life, and he's got orders to evict a diner owner from his family's building. But when he meets Madison, the charming woman running the diner, he realizes that he has a real shot of helping her keep her business. If only he can keep his motives a secret.

But as feelings begin to develop, will Madison and Jake find a way to come together in order to save the diner, and themselves?

SNOWFLAKE WISHES

SNEAK PEEK: CHAPTER ONE

I saw the object flying right before it hit me square in the face.

"Watch out!" a masculine voice yelled from the other side of the street.

His warning was too late. Struck between the eyes by the small, but hard object, I dropped the box of Christmas decorations I'd been clutching and fell flat on my back, the wind leaving me in one quick swoop.

My lungs searched for air as I lay sprawled on the sidewalk, my eyelids heavy and thick. A headache formed instantly between my eyes and I blinked slowly as a sparkly silver object came into focus on the cement beside me. My tinsel garland, of course. I blinked away the fog threatening to descend on me, the trash can next to me and tree branches above it slowly coming into focus. My nose throbbed and tears sprang to my eyes, blurring my vision and the man that was now leaning over me.

"I am so sorry!" he said, picking up the errant Christmas decorations and shoving them back in the box. "I didn't think that through."

I sat up slowly, pushing away the strong hands that gripped my shoulders. "I'm fine," I lied. I was fairly positive my nose was broken and this idiot was to blame. My hands came up to gingerly cup my nose and I winced involuntarily, eliciting a frown from the man squatting beside me. Warm, gooey blood seeped from my nostrils and covered my fingers.

The stranger pulled a handkerchief from his pocket and shoved it at me. I balled it up and pressed it to my nose. I couldn't help but notice his expensive watch. What kind of man carried around a handkerchief? A rich one did.

"Please, let me drive you to the hospital." He glanced around, obviously unfamiliar with the area. "We should get someone to look at your nose."

We did not get strangers often in our small town of Holly Springs. When we did, they were either adventurers stopping for gas, or lost tourists in need of directions to one of the larger ski resorts they were heading to.

"That's really not necessary," I said, coming to a stand. I felt fine. Aside from the probably broken nose and fuzzy feeling in my brain, naturally. And the blood. I glanced down at my shirt and groaned. It was never going to come out. Somehow it had even managed to drip on the short apron tied around my waist.

He reached forward as though he meant to steady me and I pushed away his hands. Why was he constantly touching me? Uncomfortable, I stepped away. "But thanks anyway."

He scoffed. "I can't just leave you like this. At least come in and sit down a minute." He gestured toward The Bell behind us. "This place looks quiet."

I clenched my jaw. He didn't know; he couldn't. I leaned down and picked up my box with one arm, keeping the other pressed to my nose. My voice came out nasally. "Yeah, it's quiet."

He stepped forward, his longs legs crossing the distance in one stride, and held the door for me. I set the box on the floor and took a seat at a booth along the back wall. The blood seemed to have slowed. I grabbed a napkin from the table and pressed it to my nose, shoving the sodden handkerchief into my apron pocket.

He slid in opposite of me, his dark eyebrows pulled together in concern. Combine his angular jawline and piercing blue eyes, and I had a veritable romance novel cover model on my hands. Perhaps *that* was what he was doing around here—an on-location photo shoot.

Honestly, a man this conventionally handsome could not be anything but a model. His shoulders were too broad and eyes too blue for much of anything to be going on in that perfectly styled head of his.

"What was it that hit me?" I asked, a headache forming above my eyes.

He grimaced. "A bottle of hot sauce. I was aiming for the trash can."

"From across the street?"

He had the grace to look chastised. He glanced away, giving me a view of his profile—he even looked perfect from the side. If he was not a cover model for romance novels yet, then he really should be. He could make a killing in that field.

"Wow," he said under his breath. "The service here is something else, isn't it?"

"I'm sure they've got a good reason for taking their time." I glanced around the small diner, trying to see it from an outsider's perspective. It was quiet, yes. But it was also simple, and lovely, and rich in history. But then again, I was biased.

"If I yell out to Duke do you think he'll answer?" He indicated the framed photo on the wall behind the counter. It hung beside the award for Best Diner in Town, with the name Duke Bell typed in the winner's line. "No wonder this place is empty. No one is working."

I stiffened. Reminding myself that this stranger knew nothing and would shortly be gone forever, I pasted a smile on my face. "Are you hungry?"

"Actually, yes. I went into that market down the street but all I got was an energetic sales pitch on the guy's homemade hot sauce. I bought a bottle just to get him off my back." He laughed. "Then I escaped."

"Fred."

"Excuse me?"

I kept the annoyance from my face. Or, I tried to. "That guy's name is Fred and he runs the market. The market where he sells his homemade hot sauce."

Hot sauce which this guy used to break my nose.

I stood, my irritation nearing a breaking point. The bell rang over the door. I glanced at the entrance and caught Britney's eye before turning back to the stranger and pulling a notepad from my apron pocket. "What can I get you?"

His eyes bulged as he took in my apron for seemingly the first time. "You work here?"

"You could say that."

He was either dumbfounded or working really hard to recall every point of our conversation where he'd talked about my diner. I shoved the napkin in my pocket, the blood seemed to have stopped for now, and tapped my pen on the pad while I waited. Britney took a seat at the bar behind me and my false smile stretched further the longer I waited.

He cleared his throat and turned to face me, his arm lying lazily across the back of the bench. "Do you have a decent soup selection?"

"I'm not sure what qualifies as decent, but I've got a French Onion today and a corn chowder."

"I'll take a French dip sandwich then."

"Soup?"

"French Onion."

"Drink?" I asked.

"Coke."

I pivoted away, sliding behind the counter and giving Britney exasperated eyes. I caught my messy reflection in the picture frame on the wall and dipped a fresh napkin in a cup of water before wiping the dried blood from my face.

Britney looked over her shoulder and turned back to me, her sleek blonde eyebrows raised in question. I tried to silently convey that I would not be discussing the stranger *while* he was sitting in my diner. I filled a glass with Diet Coke and placed it in front of her with a straw before starting the sandwich on the stove against the wall.

Whether from sheer stubbornness or an effort to assuage my pride, I delivered the best French dip sandwich and soup I had ever made with a fresh Coke and a side of hot fries.

"I didn't order the fries," he said when I placed the plate in front of him on the table.

"On the house."

"Oh, but I don't…"

I looked at him expectantly. He didn't what? Want them? I tried to smile, growing less patient as the headache grew more pronounced. The ring of the bell above the door saved him from answering and I left him to eat in peace as I seated Mrs. Hansen and began brewing her regular mug of tea.

I delivered the mug with a side of plain rye toast—there really was no accounting for taste sometimes.

"Madison, you've a little something right there," Mrs. Hansen said, pointing to the bridge of her own wrinkled nose.

Instinctively I reached up to touch the bridge of mine and regretted it instantly. "It's probably a bruise," I explained. "Let me know if I can get you anything else."

Safe behind the counter again, I slumped forward, resting on my elbows.

Britney peered at me over the rim of her cup, her head tilting to the side, her eyes squinting.

"That bad, huh?" I asked, my voice low and nasally.

"Um," she said. "No?"

"I just hope it doesn't turn into two big black eyes."

Britney grinned, loudly sipping the dregs of her Diet Coke. "You could always reschedule your date with Patrick."

I groaned. "I can't, though. I've rescheduled three times already and I need his help moving my furniture."

"I'm going to tell him you only want him for his body."

"Don't you dare," I said, laughing. "But I might need to borrow a little concealer."

"Girl, you're going to need more than a little."

A throat cleared to the side of the counter and I straightened. The cover model was standing a few feet away, hands in his jacket pockets. That was quick.

"Can I get you something else?"

"No, it was great. I left cash on the table."

"Wonderful. Thanks for stopping in," I said, trying very hard not to sound sarcastic. "If you're ever back in Holly Springs be sure to stop by The Bell."

He gave me a look that clearly said he knew I was delivering my spiel with a side of sarcasm.

He nodded and left.

"Explain," Britney said before the door had even closed all the way behind the guy.

I shrugged. "Nothing to say."

Her face was a picture of doubt. "There's a handsome stranger eating in your diner that you seem to have a strong dislike for and you're sporting a bruised nose. There's a story here."

"He hit me in the face with a bottle of Fred's hot sauce." I raised my hands to stave off her indignation. "It was an accident, but then he had the gall to insult my diner."

"Ah, I see," she said, leaning back on her stool. "And he's only passing through?"

"Probably," I said, removing her empty glass and wiping the counter to remove water rings. Hardly anyone passed through anymore, and when they did, they never stayed long. It was something which would need to change if I was going to save the diner.

Britney sighed. "I hope you're wrong."

Ignoring her, I moved around the counter to clear Hot Sauce Guy's table. The full plate of fries sat untouched. Scoffing, I dumped the plate in the clean-up bin with the rest of the dirty dishes.

"My boyfriend is constantly out of town and I need some eye candy. We could use some fresh men," she said, spinning around on her stool. "Especially if they look like him. They don't make them like that in Holly Springs."

ABOUT THE AUTHOR

Kasey Stockton is a staunch lover of all things romantic. She doesn't discriminate between genres and enjoys a wide variety of happily ever afters. Drawn to the Regency period at a young age when gifted a copy of *Sense and Sensibility* by her grandmother, Kasey initially began writing Regency romances. She has since written in a variety of genres, but all of her titles fall under clean romance. A native of northern California, she now resides in Texas with her own prince charming and their three children. When not reading, writing, or binge-watching chick flicks, she enjoys running, cutting hair, and anything chocolate.